I0619091

MARRYING NOEL

BRIDES OF CLEARWATER: BOOK 6

MELANIE D. SNITKER

DALLIONE MEDIA, LLC

Marrying Noel
Brides of Clearwater: Book 6
By Melanie D. Snitker

All rights reserved
© 2024 Melanie D. Snitker

Dallionz Media, LLC
P.O. Box 5283
Abilene, TX 79608

All rights reserved. No part of this publication may be reproduced, distributed, or transmitted in any form or by any means, including photocopying, recording, or other electronic or mechanical methods, without the prior written permission of the author, except in the case of brief quotations embodied in critical reviews and certain other noncommercial uses permitted by copyright law.

Please only purchase authorized editions.

For permission requests, please contact the author at the email below or through her website.

Melanie D. Snitker
melanie@melaniedsnitker.com
www.melaniedsnitker.com

This is a work of fiction. Names, characters, businesses, places, events, and incidents either are the products of the author's imagination or used in a fictitious manner. Any resemblance to actual persons, living or dead, or actual events is purely coincidental.

For Matthew Allison
Thanks for being such an
amazing brother and friend.
I love you!

1

---

oel Echolls visually perused the Monday column in her planner. With one section of the column dedicated to her personal life and another to work, it was the perfect way to keep everything organized. The fresh week—complete with fall stickers and matching washi tape—brought a smile to her face. She intended to use seasonal and Thanksgiving stickers to decorate each week throughout November. A book of Christmas stickers waited, and it would not be brought out until December first. As far as Noel was concerned, Christmas needed to wait its turn.

She loved having her week planned out. Not only did it bring order to her personal life, but her ability to schedule things as far out as possible was what landed her the job as coordinator for the Clearwater Parks and Recreation Center almost two years ago.

It was her job to be creative, come up with events to get the community engaged, plan how those events would go, and then assign people to carry them out to perfection. In other words, she worked behind the scenes. Exactly where she preferred to be.

Not that she didn't talk to other people. Of course, she did.

However, having to go business to business and convince the owners to join in different events was not her cup of tea. Not to mention dealing with the public when the events were actually taking place.

Noel much preferred to keep things running from the shadows. And that's why this job was truly the best of both worlds. It got her out in their small Texas town, gave her a say in the different activities that she scheduled for all ages, and then she got to watch as those activities came to fruition under the direct guidance of others.

Her checklist confirmed it'd been a busy day so far, and she still had many things to accomplish before the workday ended. First on that list was verifying that the last of the businesses around the town square had agreed to decorate and participate. They weren't required to, but people came from miles away to shop the square, and the more decorations, the better.

Recommending that store owners add Christmas cheer to their shops was Elsie's job.

The bubbly woman had her fingers on the pulse of the town and knew just about everyone. Seriously. If someone could sweet talk a business owner into buying an ad, putting up decorations, or donating something for a door prize, it was Elsie.

Noel slid her planner into the messenger bag that went everywhere with her. She smoothed her tan slacks, straightened the floral blouse with quarter-length sleeves she wore, and settled the messenger bag strap over her shoulder before scanning the room for Elsie.

Instead, she saw her boss, Arlene, headed her way. "Oh, Noel! Do you have a minute?"

After a glance at her watch, Noel confirmed she had exactly five to spare and would still be able to keep up with her schedule. "Sure." She turned to find the older woman's hair in mild disarray and the lines at the corners of her eyes more deeply etched than normal. "What's going on, Arlene?"

"Elsie left."

Noel blinked at her, waiting for the punchline. She did a quick scan of the large room they were in, half expecting Elsie to walk out laughing. "What?" Noel mentally went over the last two or three weeks and couldn't remember any conversations hinting at Elsie quitting her job. "Why? She didn't even give notice?"

Arlene shook her head, her silver hair shifting around her ears. "She had a family emergency. Her granddaughter is on bed rest, her daughter just had major surgery, and Elsie decided to fly over to Tennessee to help them for the rest of the year. With any luck, she'll be back in January." She gave Noel a sympathetic look.

Noel certainly couldn't fault Elsie for making that decision. The office wouldn't be the same without her. But her co-worker's absence meant something else as well. "Where are we on the Moonlight Stroll? Who's heading up A Country Christmas?"

Arlene flinched.

No. No, no, no. Please, God. This can't be happening.

Noel's chest tightened, and her neck warmed. Coordinating events was one thing, but setting up an event was something else entirely. Elsie's ability to sweet-talk people and be a friend to all was *not* a skill that they shared. "There has to be someone else."

"Not this late in the game. And not with the ability to keep things on track like you do." Arlene offered an encouraging smile. "If there was another option…"

Noel wanted to argue. Suggest someone else for the job. But Arlene was right. With Elsie gone and plans for Clearwater's two biggest events of the year already in the works, there wasn't time to hire someone else. Not and expect them to jump right in.

She smothered a groan. "Yeah. I know." She pictured the week's spread in her planner—the one that'd looked perfectly organized not ten minutes ago. A tornado might as well have ripped right through it for all the good it did her now. "Did she leave anything behind that will give me an idea of where she left off?"

Arlene's face relaxed a little. She nodded and motioned for Noel to follow her. On Elsie's desk across the room rested a green notebook. The cover was well worn, with multicolored tabs sticking out from the side. "She said this is for you."

In case there was any doubt, a sticky note curled away from the notebook. Noel reached down and smoothed it out to read,

Noel,
Everything you need is in here.
I believe in you—you've got this.
Elsie

"That makes one of us," Noel mumbled. She forced a smile for Arlene and picked up the notebook. "I'll go through this and see where we're at."

Arlene seemed happy with that and walked away.

Noel, on the other hand, tried to ignore the anxiety gnawing at her stomach as she took the notebook to her own desk. The rolling chair let out a tiny squeak as it accepted her weight. She stared at the notebook. The way the tabs were unevenly spread out along the side alone was enough to give her hives. At least each one was labeled.

"Please let it be even more organized on the inside than it looks on the outside."

She used the first tab titled "Overall" to open it.

Elsie's flowing script filled page after page with everything she needed to accomplish for the two events. There were probably thirty or forty things listed, and maybe fifteen had a check mark beside them. The good news was that most of these were things Noel had come up with herself; they were just up to Elsie to arrange or organize.

Or they had been.

Now, they were up to Noel.

She took time to look through the records on activities, entertainment, and participating businesses.

Footsteps neared, and a cup of coffee was placed at Noel's elbow. She looked up to find Arlene watching her.

"So? What's the damage?"

"Honestly?" Noel took a fortifying sip of the dark brew and let the warmth soak into her very soul. "She kept records of everything. She left a letter, too, explaining what she was going to do next." It wasn't organized like *she* would have done it, but she could go through and do that tonight.

She could just hear her twin brother, Jace, telling her to leave the notebook alone and not add stress to her life. It was hard to explain how not having everything organized just right did that anyway. At least Jace understood more than most people did.

"I'll help where I can," Arlene offered. "I'm sorry this got dumped on you out of nowhere."

"It's okay. What doesn't kill us makes us stronger, right?"

Great, now that song by Kelly Clarkson was going to be playing over and over in her head all day.

Arlene smiled and left Noel to her work.

Noel opened her own planner and laid it on the desk beside Elsie's notebook.

"Okay, God," she began in a whispered prayer. "This right here is more than I can deal with right now. Please help me sort through this mess."

Trying to combine everything was going to be a nightmare. For now, she needed to tackle everything that had to get done today.

Fifteen minutes later, she had her list.

Goose bumps peppered the exposed skin on her arms as she stepped out of the building and into the slightly cooler air. Sometimes it took a while for fall to catch up in this area of Texas, but this change in temperature hinted that they'd all be seeing more of it soon.

Elsie had two different meetings arranged this morning with businesses on the square. But first, Noel needed to stop by Clara's Café to see if her friend, Clara, was willing to donate muffins for the breakfast crafting event at the senior center. The café was on the same side of the street as the town hall but about five buildings down. Noel headed in that direction.

This was another thing she liked about her job—and Clearwater in general. Everything was close by. Noel made it a point to walk as much as possible. Rarely did she get home in the evening with fewer than 15,000 steps.

Which was why, no matter what outfit she wore, a good pair of sneakers were a must.

The moment Noel stepped into the café, the tantalizing scent of baked goods fought for her attention. The glass case showcasing the variety of sweets drew Noel over. Nearly everything in there looked amazing, but it was the cinnamon scone that had her mouth watering.

And that's when Mother's voice echoed in her head. *"You don't need carbs, Noel. Your natural body type isn't on your side anyway. At your age, it's easy to gain weight."* Way to make being thirty five years old feel old.

Noel had taken her mother's criticism to heart as a child and teen but had since been able to push it aside. Or at least ignore it, for the most part.

"Hey, Noel. It's good to see you. Can I interest you in a cookie?" Clara approached the counter, her dark hair pulled into a thick bun at the back of her head with tendrils curling near her cheeks. Her dark eyes lit up, along with her friendly smile.

"Actually, I think that cinnamon scone over there is calling my name." Noel pointed. She thought about what her mother would say and chuckled. "In fact, go ahead and bag one of those for me, would you, please?"

"Absolutely." Using a pair of metal tongs, Clara easily slid the scone into a paper bag, folded the top over, and handed it across the counter. "Here you go."

"Thank you." Noel withdrew her wallet and gave her some money. "So, I was wondering if I could talk to you about the breakfast over at the senior center the first week of December."

Clara offered a knowing smile. "You can count me in for the muffins. Mrs. Dawson has already asked me twice if my muffins will be there. I wouldn't want to disappoint the fans."

Noel laughed. Mrs. Dawson was one of the more outspoken women at the senior center. She would do anything for anyone but wasn't the least bit afraid to speak her mind. "Fantastic. Thanks, Clara. I'll put the café down as one of our main sponsors, then." She slipped the scone into her messenger bag. She couldn't wait to eat it as a treat after lunch. "Are you going to make the cranberry scones again in December?"

"Absolutely." Clara leaned a hip against the counter. "I've got a new recipe for an eggnog scone, too, that I'm going to try. You want to be one of my taste testers?"

"I'd be hurt if you didn't ask me." Noel absolutely loved everything eggnog. Another food that her mother would highly disapprove of. "I can't wait to try it." She glanced at her watch. "I'd better run. Thanks again for the scone and for the muffins next month. Have a great afternoon!"

"You, too!" Clara waved before turning her attention to a customer who passed Noel on the way into the café.

Well, that was easy. Noel marked that task off her mental list.

Which meant it was time to visit Mr. Brooks. He was an older gentleman who was set in his ways. He was also quite cranky, and Elsie was the only one at the Parks & Rec office who could speak to him and still come out with a smile.

Mr. Brooks owned a store filled with all kinds of antique toys and games. Where he lacked tact with adults, he could charm children like good old St. Nick himself.

Every year, Elsie set off to convince Mr. Brooks to decorate the outside of his store to match the theme chosen for the town. And every year, he protested. Sometimes, he outright refused.

Truthfully, Noel thought they should let the poor guy be. But Arlene wanted him to get on board this year since they were going with an oversized toy theme.

"Lord, give me the patience I know I'm going to need for this." Noel took in a fortifying breath and crossed the street. Mr. Brooks' Collectibles was as boring on the outside as it was exciting on the inside. There were no decorations around the windows or on the door. There wasn't even a fun "Open" sign hanging outside.

But the moment Noel pulled the door open and entered, she was surrounded by her childhood. Truth be told, she and Jace probably had more toys than most kids their age simply because their parents piled them on in place of quality time or attention. Looking around, Noel was convinced she and Jace could've combined their toys and opened their own store back then.

Since it was the middle of the morning and school was still going, there was little activity in the store. It was easy to find Mr. Brooks by the register, carefully lining up old Micro Machines on display.

He scowled the moment he saw her, the lines in his forehead deepening. "I see Elsie sent you to do her dirty work this time, huh?"

"Actually, Elsie had a family emergency and went to help out for the rest of the year." Noel didn't feel it was her place to share more than that. But she certainly wasn't going to let Mr. Brooks speak ill of Elsie, either.

A flash of concern crossed Mr. Brooks' features. "I'm sorry to hear that." But the emotion didn't last long. He squinted at her. "You may as well know that I have no intention of decorating the outside of my store. I don't need to. People come in to buy gifts anyway."

Noel wanted to let it go. Especially when he fixed her with a glare that dared her to contradict him. She had a long line of situations just like this ahead of her, and she may as well face it head-on.

"I understand that. But since we're decorating the square with oversized toys, we thought it'd be perfect to position large toy soldiers outside your store. Maybe on each side of the door? You could hang one of your large airplane models over the doorway, too." She tilted her head toward the three different aircraft that were sitting on top of a shelf. They'd been there for as long as she could remember. Were they even for sale? She imagined Mr. Brooks himself flying them when he was a little boy.

Mr. Brooks had started shaking his head before she'd even finished talking. "I'm not interested."

"I can have someone do all the work, Mr. Brooks. You won't have to lift a finger. Just say the word."

"No." He fixed her with a look that told her, under no uncertain terms, that he was finished with the conversation.

Noel gave him a nod, forcing herself to act casual. "If you change your mind, please let me know. Have a good day, Mr. Brooks." There was no return farewell as Noel made her way out of the store and back onto the sidewalk outside.

She had no doubt Elsie would have attempted to change the man's mind at least one or two more times. Noel, however, was no stranger to having someone push and push to get something they wanted. She was inclined to leave Mr. Brooks in peace. Besides, she still had quite a list of errands to accomplish before lunch.

Next was the new bookstore. Everyone in Clearwater was excited at the prospect of not having to drive into San Antonio to visit one. The business had seemed to pop up out of nowhere, and while the owner had gone through all the proper channels, this was the first time anyone from Parks and Rec had been to see them.

Noel's job was to meet the owner and see if he or she was interested in participating in both of the town's holiday events coming up. If they were going to be open before the Moonlight Stroll late Thanksgiving evening, they might need help with decoration guidelines.

And there it was again—the intense weight on her shoulders over knowing she was going to be heading this project. Maybe now was a good time to consider a change in employment.

The brick building across the street beckoned her. She waited for traffic, crossed Main quickly, and took in the printed sign taped on the inside of one of the big front windows that said "Book Haven" in large, bold letters.

Noel's cell phone rang before she could enter the establishment. Without glancing at the screen, she answered. "This is Noel."

"Imagine that. My daughter actually answered one of my calls." Leslie Echolls' voice nearly dripped with satisfaction and sarcasm.

If Noel had known her mother was on the other end of the call, she'd have sent it straight to voicemail. She stopped at a bench outside of Book Haven and set her bag down with a sigh. "I'm working, and I've got a meeting in a few minutes. What's going on?"

There was a significant pause as though Mother were trying to eke the conversation out for as long as possible. Finally, she began. "The Christmas party is just a few weeks away. I need to know who your plus one is so that I can get the name to the planner."

Noel rolled her eyes. The Echolls family Christmas party. A festive title for the yearly torture session that she and Jace were forced to endure. Never once had Noel taken a plus one, and yet her mother insisted on pointing that out. Every. Single. Year.

How about a minus one? Because the last thing Noel looked forward to during the holidays was going to her parents' Christmas party.

She used to dread Christmas completely until Jace had his little boy, Gunner. When Jace's wife, Samantha, passed away a few days after Gunner was born, it was up to Noel and Jace to make Christmas happy for Gunner. Just thinking about her five-year-old nephew brought a smile to Noel's face.

Then Jace met the love of his life. He and Bonnie got married two years ago, and Jace has been the happiest Noel had ever seen him. Add to that another baby boy born back in July, and they were the perfect family.

A family that welcomed Noel to all their celebrations and events. Something she was grateful for.

She just wished she could skip her parents' party, too. Now, that would be the cinnamon and nutmeg on top of the proverbial eggnog.

"I don't have a plus one. It's just me this year."

"Well, you'll find a plus one and give me a name in the next week, or I'll assign one to you." The announcement came with as much emotion as a computerized telemarketer.

Noel rolled her eyes. "You don't assign a date like you would a number at the DMV, Mom."

"Try me."

That tone. Noel knew it well. Her mother would make good on her threat. The idea that she would show up at the party to find a blind date waiting for her had Noel's stomach churning with nerves.

She fought to ignore her nausea. "I've got to go. I'll talk to you later."

"I'm sure that you will."

With that, the connection ended. Noel imagined her mother ending the call with a flourish and a scowl.

She tried to push the conversation from her mind. But between having Elsie's job dumped on her this morning, dealing with Mr. Brooks, and now this, it was too much for one morning.

The all-too-familiar tightening sensation began in her

chest, and Noel swallowed against the lump in her throat. *Not now, God.* She refused to have a panic attack here on Main Street in full view of anyone walking by.

Instinct took over, and she pulled open Book Haven's door. Soft chimes announced her arrival, and the scents of varnish and paper filled the air. She tried to focus on that and willed the growing panic to recede.

She leaned a shoulder against an empty wooden bookcase and tried to catch her breath. The idea of the town's new business owner seeing her like this…

A deep voice came from the back of the building. "I apologize for the mess. I'll be right there."

Noel groaned.

2

T he stack of papers in Cooper Meyer's hand felt much heavier than they should have. It was an inventory of the books he'd purchased to stock the shelves of his bookstore. Those books were stored in the countless sealed boxes scattered around the building.

It was all a wonderful culmination of the planning, saving, time, and sweat he'd put into the project over the past few years.

It was also completely overwhelming. He'd originally planned to open before Thanksgiving. The hope was that timing the grand opening with holiday shopping might start his fledgling business off on the right foot. He thought that a tentative deadline would give him plenty of time.

Then there were shipment problems. There was a leak in the roof that needed repairs. Not to mention a health scare with his mom. Praise God the surgery was a success, and the tumor on her thyroid was benign. But she still had some recovery to do.

Which meant Cooper was caring for his brother, Jett, more than normal. Not that he minded. Eventually, he planned to take over the full-time care that his disabled younger brother needed. It's just that the timing wasn't necessarily the best.

As it was, it would take a small miracle to open in time for Christmas, much less Thanksgiving and the potential Black Friday sales.

This bookstore had felt like an answer to prayers. But there'd been several times in the last few weeks where he'd wondered if he'd been on the wrong track. It'd be nice if things would calm down a bit so he could catch his breath a little.

Cooper ran a hand through his close-cropped, dark hair and scratched at his short goatee. Standing there staring at the invoices wasn't going to accomplish anything. Instead, he needed to take the mess of books he'd ordered and figure out how to categorize them and get them arranged in the store.

He dropped the invoices into a drawer in the corner desk of the small office and pushed it closed.

The first thing he needed to do was to arrange the heavy bookshelves that stood next to each other like giant dominoes in the main room. Once that was accomplished and a reading place assigned, it would be easier to sort through the books.

At least, that was the hope.

He was reaching for the dolly when chimes out front announced the arrival of a visitor.

Cooper had chosen not to lock the front door, but he hadn't expected anyone to drop by. Whoever it was, hopefully, they wouldn't judge the chaos they'd just walked into too harshly.

"I apologize for the mess. I'll be right there."

He dusted his hands off on his jeans and left the cozy office.

At first, he didn't see anyone else in the building. And

then he spotted a woman leaning against the end of one of the bookcases. Her head was bent forward slightly, and her long, blonde hair tumbled past her shoulders to hide her face. She had her arms crossed tightly in front of her.

He took a step toward her and stopped. "Are you okay?"

She shook her head but didn't look up.

That's when Cooper realized she was breathing quickly to the point of nearly hyperventilating.

Her arms dropped, and she rested her hands on her knees as she leaned over further.

If she didn't slow her breathing, she was going to pass out.

Cooper dashed forward and wrapped a hand around her upper arm. "Come on. You need to sit down for a minute."

He thought she was going to argue. Instead, she allowed him to lead her to a chair behind the main counter and ease her into it.

She rested her elbows on her knees as she tried to curb her breathing.

Cooper had seen his brother go through something very similar some years ago.

This woman was having a panic attack.

He looked around for a box he'd seen earlier. Spotting it, he lifted a flap and grabbed a black axolotl plush wearing a T-shirt. He placed it on the woman's knees.

"Focus on the axolotl and block everything else out. Take one breath. Then another." He spoke in a calm voice. Careful to make sure she knew he was there but to keep his distance so as not to crowd her.

Or at least that's what helped Jett when he had an attack. Thankfully, his brother hadn't had one in at least five years.

Truthfully, Cooper had no idea whether the same strategy would help in this instance.

The woman scooped up the axolotl with both hands and stared at it as her breathing steadily returned to a normal rate. She ran a thumb over the top of the plush's soft back.

When she lifted her head, a pair of beautiful blue eyes fixed on Cooper. Immediately, embarrassment clouded her features.

"I'm so sorry." She paused as though she couldn't believe what had just happened. "I wouldn't have come in if I'd known it would be that bad." She looked around the room and seemed relieved to see that there were no other witnesses.

"I'm glad you did. It'd be a lot easier to find a focal point in here than it would've been out on the sidewalk."

She seemed to concede his point. With one hand, she lifted the axolotl and pointed to the wording on its shirt. "I read olotl books. That's cute." Her voice still seemed weak, but she smiled at him then, and her entire face transformed. Those blue eyes sparkled, and it seemed to take the edge off the worry and stress. "Thank you. I take it you have experience with panic attacks?"

"Not personally, but I've helped my brother through a number of them in the past." Cooper gave her a small shrug. "Having something specific to focus on always seemed to help him. I was hoping the same would work for you."

"I appreciate it." Her face, which was pale earlier, turned a pretty pink.

There were a few moments of silence.

Cooper cleared his throat. "Was there a particular reason you came inside? Is there anything else I can help you with?"

"Oh!" She practically jumped up from the chair. The blush in her cheeks darkened. "Yes." She set the axolotl plush on the counter. "My name is Noel Echolls, and I work for Clearwater Parks and Recreation." She took in a subtle breath as though trying to re-center herself and put the panic attack behind her. "We're organizing two major holiday events for the town, and I was hoping we could count you in as a participating business."

By the time she'd finished talking, Noel seemed to have transitioned from being panicked to calm and focused. She moved to retrieve a messenger bag from the floor next to the bookcase where he'd originally found her. Cooper hadn't even noticed the bag before.

She pulled a flyer out with "Moonlight Stroll" written across the top. He'd seen one on a window next door and was familiar with the event from years past. Even still, he scanned the flyer for information.

Noel continued her explanation of the event. "It starts at nine o'clock on Thanksgiving night. Any stores participating will be open with extra Christmas lights lighting the way. It invites people who enjoy the Black Friday experience to shop locally. There will be cookie and hot chocolate stations available as well."

Cooper nodded. "I've heard about the event in the past." He wasn't one to go out late on Thanksgiving, though. He usually had his Christmas shopping done by then. But he had to admit, it'd be a great way to introduce the bookstore to the community. "I would love to participate, but I'm not sure I'll have the store ready by then." He waved a hand toward the disarray around them.

With a critical eye, Noel took in the piles of boxes, the display shelves that hadn't been properly set up yet, and the three comfortable chairs that were still wrapped in plastic.

When she faced him again, she looked thoughtful. Without saying another word, she again dug into her messenger bag and pulled out a colorful book with rings that matched instead of the typical binder.

She opened it and flipped to a page. When she laid it

down flat, a calendar for the month of November was visible, complete with cheerful stickers and plenty of hand-written notes.

Noel studied it for several moments, then flipped several pages to the December calendar. In between, Cooper caught sight of extremely detailed and organized lists and daily schedules.

Impressive.

"What we could do is not make your store official on our list of participating businesses. But if you're able to open in time for the Moonlight Stroll, people will find it as they wander the square." She tapped squares between the two calendars as she silently counted. "Then you would have almost two and a half weeks between that and the Christmas Countdown event. Now that one we print a map for, so you'll definitely want to let me know as soon as possible if you'd like to participate."

She looked at him then, her expression hopeful. If she was even half as organized as her planner suggested, she probably had all of her I's dotted and T's crossed long before it was necessary.

How did he explain that his life was somewhat unpredictable right now without going into the entire story about his brother or his mom's surgery?

Sure, in theory, everything Noel suggested ought to come together. But in reality, Cooper recognized that things weren't always so cut and dried.

He hardly knew this woman, and yet the idea of telling her that he couldn't commit to the events and possibly disappointing her bothered him a great deal.

Cooper pointed to her planner. "I take it you like to stay organized."

She bristled a little as though she'd been teased about it in the past. "Yes, I do." Her back straightened. "I actually keep one for work, one for home, and a separate one for my finances."

The tone of her voice didn't really change, but the friendly, hopeful look in her eyes dulled a little.

"I mean no disrespect. At all. I find it admirable." He held up both hands, hoping she believed he had nothing but good intentions. "Take a look around, and you'll quickly find that organization is not my strong point." He paused. "In fact, I don't suppose you'd be interested in a very short-term evening job helping me organize this mess and getting the store ready to open, would you?"

The suggestion poured out of his mouth before his brain caught up with itself. What was he thinking? She obviously had a full-time job already. Why would she be willing to spend her evenings going through box after box of books? He was about to apologize and take the offer back when she spoke.

Her response was immediate. "I'd be very interested."

She seemed as surprised by her answer as he was by the original offer.

"Okay." They stared at each other for several heartbeats. "What time are you free in the evenings?"

"I get off work at five. I'd need to run home, change clothes, and grab something to eat. I could be here as early as six."

That meant she didn't live too far away. It would also give him plenty of time to pick up Jett and bring him back to the store before then, too.

"That sounds great." He told her how much he'd pay per hour and was relieved when she agreed to the wage.

She took another look at her planner. "I'd be able to help this entire week, Saturday, and then through Tuesday of next week. But I'll need to reserve Wednesday evening for last-minute things related to the Stroll."

Surely, seven evenings and the bulk of Saturday would be enough to get this place up and running. "That sounds good. Then I'll see you this evening."

He held out a hand. The moment her much smaller palm touched his, he was keenly aware of the physical connection. His heart jolted, and Cooper forced himself to let go of her hand in a timely fashion.

"Thank you. For the job and for earlier." Noel shouldered her messenger bag and took a step back. The confidence on her face while she was explaining the town events was replaced by an obvious nervousness. With an awkward wave of a hand, she left the store.

Cooper stared at the door as it slowly closed behind her.

Seriously, what just happened? A half hour ago, he was trying to figure out how he was going to get everything done.

"That was an interesting solution, God," he said aloud with a chuckle.

Now he had a new, very short-term employee after handing her a plush axolotl who was wearing a shirt so she wouldn't have a full-on panic attack in his store.

Seeing how well-organized Noel was for her job gave him hope that she might actually be able to get the store inventory under control.

But truth be told, when Noel exited the store a few moments ago, she left behind some questions that Cooper couldn't stop pondering. Like why she was so eager to nab a second job. Or why she had been experiencing a panic attack in the first place.

3

The moment Noel entered her home and shut the door behind her, she breathed a deep sigh of relief. She'd survived the rest of her day at work, put out more fires than she cared to count, and had less than an hour before she needed to leave again for her new part-time job.

She had her hands full dealing with Elsie's tasks. What on earth possessed her to accept Cooper's offer to work at the bookstore in the evenings?

Normally, she looked forward to the solitude she found in the home she'd purchased two years ago. Either that or going over to Jace's house and spending time with his family. There was no better end to the day than playing with Gunner or cuddling his four-month-old brother, Grayson.

Noel thought over the whole bookstore fiasco, and her cheeks immediately warmed. What a horrible way to introduce herself to someone new.

What must Cooper have thought about her when he found her freaking out in his store? She pictured the axolotl with the T-shirt and chuckled before she groaned.

So embarrassing.

But she had to hand it to him. Focusing on the plush had helped.

She just hoped that he really had offered her the job because he'd been impressed by her organizational abilities and not because he felt sorry for her or was trying to distract her from her panic.

His job offer had been spontaneous. What if she showed up tonight, and he'd changed his mind?

The possibility annoyed her. And then she reminded herself that she'd have her precious evening downtime back.

She had barely changed into a more casual long-sleeved shirt to go with her jeans when her phone rang. Jace's name popped up on the screen.

Noel smiled as she answered. "Hey. How's your day been?"

"Busy. I had to replace a whole section of fencing on the north side this afternoon. That last storm we had knocked a tree into it. I'm lucky we didn't lose any stock."

Jace had taken over the sheep ranch their grandfather had left the two of them in his will. Noel and Jace had wonderful memories of spending summers with their grandparents at that ranch, but they had both been shocked when Grandpa left it to them after he passed.

It'd been a huge change for Jace when he'd decided to quit his hectic job and move out to the ranch with Gunner. Gunner's weekday nanny, Bonnie, had gone with them and lived in the apartment above the garage. Noel had moved in temporarily, too, in order to help with Gunner on the weekends.

Until Jace finally admitted he was in love with Bonnie. Once the two of them got married, Noel wanted to give the new family some space.

That's when she decided to leave behind the impersonal

apartment she'd been renting and buy a house near the town square.

The location was perfect. She was within walking distance of work, shopping, and even a small grocery store three blocks away. The house wasn't huge, but it had a lot of character. And since Noel owned it, she could do whatever she wanted with it.

"I'm glad you got the fencing fixed and that you didn't lose any sheep." The powerful thunderstorm that hit a couple of days ago had taken the whole town by surprise. Storms like that were rare in November.

"What about you? How was your Monday?"

Noel chuckled. As she dumped a can of soup into a saucepan and turned on the heat, she told Jace about Elsie leaving without notice and having to pick up the slack.

She also told him about her phone conversation with their mother but left out the panic attack. If she shared that detail, it would make him even more upset with their mother.

"So don't go." Jace's voice was firm. The suggestion was simple.

Except things were never that simple when it came to their parents.

"You know that's not an option." If she didn't go, their parents would dump all their anger and disappointment on Jace and Bonnie. At least when Noel was there, the disapproval could be split three ways.

"It absolutely is. For that matter, maybe we need to take a stand, and none of us go. They don't own us, Noel."

"I know." They'd had this conversation before. Their parents had been furious when they didn't sell their grandparents' farm and split the money four ways with them. They were disappointed when Jace married "the help" and when Noel chose to work a "menial" job.

Going to the Christmas party once a year out of respect was something the siblings had discussed years ago. As much as they both dreaded it, it was one night a year. Survivable.

Noel absently stirred the soup. The clattering sound as the spoon hit the edge of the saucepan filled in the silence on the phone.

Finally, Jace spoke again.

"Do you want me to see if I have a friend that'll go with us?"

Her. He meant as a date for her.

"Thanks. I'll handle it. Even if I have to let Mom pair me up with someone I don't know, it's only for one night. I don't have to ever see him again. I'll survive."

She could feel her brother's disapproval, but he wisely said nothing.

It was time to change the subject. "I got a part-time evening job."

As she poured the bubbling soup into a large bowl and sat on a stool at the small bar that bordered her kitchen, Noel told Jace about the bookstore.

"It sounds like I'll get to help decide where the books will be displayed and organize them." It was like setting up a planner but on a much grander scale. She hoped she wasn't thinking too much of the job. She should probably wait until she spoke with Cooper tonight to see what he really expected her to do.

"It definitely sounds like it's right up your alley," Jace agreed. "I just don't want you to over-commit yourself, especially since you're dealing with Elsie's job now. And aren't you volunteering at Joyful Hope, too?"

Bonnie's brother, Wyatt Tabor, owned a horse stable that he'd turned into a place where people with special needs and seniors could go for hippotherapy and so much more. Wyatt had a series of holiday-themed activities planned for the public throughout the rest of the year, and Noel had happily volunteered to help with several of them.

If there was one thing she wasn't giving up, it was helping out at the stables. Still, knowing how much Jace worried about her warmed Noel's heart. "I'm good, Jace. But thank you."

"Well, I was originally calling to see if you wanted to join us for dinner tonight. How about lunch after church on Sunday instead?"

Noel grinned. "Sold. I'll be looking forward to it."

"Me, too. And Noel?" He paused just long enough to make sure she was listening. "I'm serious when I say don't let Mom stress you out this year. It's better to bow out of the party and deal with the consequences than it is to end up sick."

Noel cringed. One year, everything had been so stressful that she'd ended up with frequent panic attacks on top of getting the flu. It had taken weeks to fully recover. It was the only year she did miss the Christmas party, and their parents had never let her forget it.

"I promise I'll talk to you if it gets that bad."

"I'm going to hold you to that."

They said their goodbyes, and Noel hung up. She looked at the bowl of soup sitting in front of her. Much of the steam had drifted away, and she hadn't eaten a single bite yet. She took a tentative sip. It was still plenty warm enough to eat, which she did in record time.

Before heading back out, she made sure she had everything she needed in her messenger bag. She preferred to walk, but this time of the year, the sun was going down by seven, and she didn't want to walk back in the dark. Instead, she got in her car and drove the four blocks to the bookstore.

As she parked and approached the store, the excitement and confidence she felt earlier began to break apart, quickly replaced with uncertainty. With a steadying breath, she pulled the door open to the sound of chimes announcing her presence.

She'd expected to find Cooper inside.

Instead, a younger man with dark hair and a narrow face looked up from his spot at the main counter. His brown eyes lit up with interest, and he hopped off the chair and rushed in her direction.

"Welcome. Welcome. Come in. Come inside." He firmly grasped her hand in his and tugged her in the direction of a small stack of books on one of the closest bookshelves. "You want to buy a book?" He didn't quite look her in the eyes as he chose one from the shelf and handed it to her, a triumphant smile on his face.

"Jett, buddy, you need to give her a little space." Cooper entered the room then, and his voice caught the younger man's attention. "It's always good to welcome someone when they come into the store, but you can't touch them. Remember, use your words, not your hands."

Cooper gave Noel an apologetic look. She had been taken aback at first, but it was clear the younger man had some form of special needs. She'd helped several people in a similar situation while volunteering for Wyatt's organization. She gave Cooper a subtle nod, which seemed to surprise him.

"Like this," Cooper continued as he turned to Noel. "Hello. Welcome to our store. Make yourself comfortable, and let me know if you need anything."

"Thank you so much," Noel returned.

Cooper looked at the other man. "Then we let the customer look at books and decide on her own if she wants to buy something. And remember, it's okay if she doesn't because she might come back on a different day. Or the next person who comes in might want to buy something instead."

"Yes. Okay." The younger man nodded. He reached out and took the book back from Noel and put it on the shelf again.

Cooper put a hand on the thin man's shoulder. "This is my brother, Jett. Jett, this is Noel. She's going to help us get the store ready for real customers. Isn't that great?"

"That's great," Jett repeated. He looked at her face directly for a second or two before turning away. "That's great." He went back to the counter and whatever he was working on when she came in.

After locking the front door and closing the blinds, Cooper subtly motioned for Noel to follow him into the small office at the back.

"I apologize. I intended to be out here with Jett when you came in."

"It's fine. Really." While she'd been surprised by his actions, she quickly understood the situation. Or at least had an idea of what was going on.

"Most people are taken aback when something like that happens. But you weren't." He studied her for several moments, his dark eyes focused on her face. "I take it you know someone with an intellectual disability?"

"Not well. But my sister-in-law's brother owns Joyful Hope Stables. They have a lot to offer individuals with disabilities. I've volunteered there many times in the past."

Cooper nodded, clearly impressed. "I have to admit, I'm happy to hear that because Jett will be here in the evenings more often than not." He glanced into the main part of the store and seemed satisfied to see that his brother was still content at the counter. "Jett has Fragile X Syndrome. Some doctors have suggested that he may have autism as well, although it's difficult to tell where one might end and the other begins. He still lives with our parents and probably will for a while. However, he will eventually move in with me and I'll be his primary caregiver. So we're slowly trying to increase the time that we spend together outside of our parents' home." He motioned to the space around them. "I'm opening this bookstore for both of us. It'll give us a place where we can work together. Where I can help him focus on building skills and having a job."

"I think that's great," Noel told him sincerely. She'd heard many stories from Wyatt about families who struggled to transition when their disabled children reached adulthood and continued to need frequent help and guidance. "Jett is lucky to have such a wonderful and supportive family. And especially a brother willing to stand by him and plan ahead like that." Her admiration for Cooper jumped up a notch or two.

The slightest tint of red colored the tips of Cooper's ears. He scratched the back of his neck. "Yeah, well. He's family, and you do what you need to do. Know what I mean?"

"I know exactly what you mean."

EARLIER IN THE EVENING, Cooper had been afraid that Noel might be uncomfortable around Jett. His brother was sweet, and he thrived on being around other people. But he also had no real understanding of personal space. It was a lot for some individuals.

As soon as Cooper realized that not only had Jett been holding Noel's hand, but had given her a book to buy, Cooper had been sure she would change her mind about working there in the evenings.

Instead, she'd seemed to accept Jett without question. It

was a rare enough quality that it was impossible for Cooper to ignore.

Two hours later, Noel sat cross-legged on the floor, her back against the counter, while she went through the inventory list with a fine-tooth comb. Meanwhile, Jett was looking at his favorite Christmas search book as he sat on the floor nearby. There wasn't much interaction between them. But occasionally, Jett would point to an object that he found and then lift the book so that Noel could see it. Most often, it was the hidden reindeer on each page.

What impressed Cooper was the fact that, when Jett did speak to her, Noel looked up from what she was doing and then commented on what Jett had to show her before going back to her work. There was no denying her seemingly natural patience with him.

Cooper had seen way too many people treat Jett as less than a person because of his intellectual disability. It warmed his heart to discover that Noel was not one of them.

It was nearly nine o'clock before Noel finally set aside the papers and stood with a groan.

"So what do you think?" he asked her.

"I think you have an impressive number of books to organize," she responded with an encouraging smile. She turned to a page in her notebook and handed it to him. "If you can pile all the boxes in rows here against the counter and get the bookshelves set up where you want them, I am confident that I can get everything organized for you."

Cooper's brows lifted. "You sound pretty sure of yourself there."

Noel shrugged and pointed to the page. According to her chart, if he held up his end of the bargain tomorrow, she projected to have all the books on shelves by the end of Saturday. That would leave him several days before the

Moonlight Stroll to take care of any last-minute things that might come up.

"I think we can do it," she said with confidence.

Her use of the word "we" was completely appropriate, given their new working relationship. Still, hearing it and feeling like he had someone else to share this burden with meant a lot. He knew that if he asked his parents, they'd be down here in a heartbeat. But Mom still needed her rest, and Dad needed to be there to take care of her.

He'd find a way to get these boxes moved tomorrow, even if he'd be feeling every single one the next day.

"Well, if you're up for the challenge, then so am I," he told her with a smile.

Her blue eyes brightened. "I'm free to work as late as you need the rest of this week. I do have commitments on Sunday, though."

"Not a problem. And when it comes to Saturday, please only stay as long as you're able to. I don't expect you to help all day."

All she did was nod her agreement.

Jett covered his mouth in a yawn, and Cooper was feeling exhausted himself. "In that case, why don't we call it a night, and I'll see you here at six tomorrow evening."

"That sounds good." Noel got everything put away in her bag and slung it over one shoulder. "It was good to meet you, Jett."

"Nice to meet you, too," he told her with a grin.

Noel turned to Cooper. "I'm looking forward to this. Thanks again for the offer to help."

"Trust me, you're doing me the favor." He unlocked the door and held it open for her. The crisp air met them in the doorway, and the holiday lights that had already been put up twinkled in the darkness. "Get home safely."

"I will. Good night."

"Good night." He watched long enough to see her get into her car before closing the door again.

Jett had gotten up from his spot at the counter and looked like he was ready to go, too. "She was a nice lady," he said.

Cooper smiled. "Yes, she was. Come on, let's get you home and in bed."

Jett nodded as he yawned again. "I'm very sleepy."

They got a few more things cleaned up, turned off the lights, and headed out.

Cooper didn't look forward to moving all the boxes. But having a chance to get to know Noel over the next week or so? Absolutely.

4

I t took all day and calling in a favor from a friend, but Cooper managed to get the book boxes stacked and the bookcases set up where he wanted them to be.

Hopefully, it will give him and Noel a chance to get a jump start on organizing categories this evening.

Noel had made a ton of notes last night. Cooper had no idea what all she wrote down, but he was curious to see what her game plan was.

He was already exhausted after moving the boxes, but it was all worth it when Noel walked in, and her jaw dropped in shock.

"Wow. It's like a whole different store." She set her bag on a chair by the counter and took in the large space. "Give me the grand tour."

"All right." He pointed to the series of bookcases that stood just below the windows that lined the front of the store. "These are for new releases and local authors. I'm hoping that, once people realize the store is here, I'll have authors coming in with their books. Maybe we can do some book signings next year."

He led her across the store, past several rows of book-cases, to a little corner. Again, bookcases that were about chest high lined both walls that bordered the area. "This is for the children's section. I want to have fun posters or special editions of books up on the walls above the bookcases. One of the chairs by the counter will come over here, and I plan to purchase a bean bag chair or two as well." He had thought about a colorful square rug to indicate where the section began and ended, too, but he'd have to see how far the money went first.

Noel smiled. "I can totally picture a children's author sitting in that chair, reading a book out loud to kids gathered around him or her on the floor."

That was exactly what he'd been thinking of, too. He grinned at her, glad that his vision for the store seemed to be at least somewhat apparent.

Cooper looked around the room. "So basically, aside from new releases and children's books, everything else will need to be organized on the other shelves. Non-fiction and fiction, which will be further divided." He pointed to the counter. "I want to have some small toys and puzzles, too. I figured having those on a display by the counter would be a good idea. People might be more inclined to grab them as gifts to go with a book."

He'd made great progress, but considering just how many books there were in the boxes, it suddenly didn't feel like that much. He shrugged. "What are your thoughts?"

"I think it all sounds great." As though she were a little kid in a toy shop trying to decide what to look at first, Noel placed her hands on her hips and slowly made a complete circle as she took it all in. With a decisive nod, she said, "All right. Let me add the location and number of bookcases, and we'll get everything figured out tonight. Hopefully, we can start working on unpacking boxes tomorrow."

With that, she strode to the counter and began to take out her planners. "Jett isn't here today?"

"He has a day program on Tuesdays and Thursdays. He goes for most of the day, and they work on life skills, job skills, and things like that. He enjoys it, but it always pushes him, and he's exhausted by the time he gets home again." Cooper watched as Noel opened the notebook she'd been writing in last night. "Since he is so tired, he usually stays home those evenings."

"That makes sense." Noel took a handful of colored pens from her bag. "I know when I'm learning something new, I come away mentally drained." She finished unpacking her things and spread them out on the counter.

"So what have you got?" he asked as he looked at the papers over her shoulder.

"I went through the inventory of books and broke them down into genres or categories and then assigned those each a color. Then, in the next column is the number of books assigned to that category." She ran a slender finger down the colorful list and handed it to him.

She'd been incredibly thorough. "It looks good to me."

"Wonderful! Okay, so I brought some paper with me. We can go through and write all the categories down, and then we can start placing them on bookcases so we know approximately where those books will go. If we write the number of books in each category, then we'll know if we need a large space or a smaller one."

It all made perfect sense. He took the chair beside her and accepted a stack of paper. "How about I start at the bottom of the list, and you start at the top?" he suggested.

When she agreed, they began making the category labels. They'd both written a few of them when she spoke again. "What were you doing before you decided to open the bookstore?"

Cooper finished writing "science fiction" in blue and set the paper aside. "I worked for a local insurance agency. It wasn't bad, but I was required to travel for a few days every other month. Every time I was gone, Jett would have night-mares and exhibit behavioral problems." And like Jett's thera-pists said, not everything in life can work the way Jett wanted it to. Sometimes, he would just have to deal with a situation and learn to cope. All of that was certainly true, but Cooper didn't like being away, either. Not from Jett. But also not from his parents. "Then, a couple of months ago, our mom started having some health concerns. It took a while and a lot of tests, but they discovered she had a tumor on her thyroid. Praise God, it was benign. She had her thyroid removed a couple of weeks ago and is doing much better now."

"But through all of that, your parents needed more help with Jett."

"Exactly." He reached for an orange pen and began to write "Travel and Leisure" on a piece of paper. "I don't want to worry about something happening while I'm away. It also made it clear to my parents and me that we need to start tran-sitioning Jett toward living with me. The fact is, my parents have been caring for him his whole life. I want them to feel free to do things together. To enjoy some form of retirement. To go on a trip, just the two of them." He stopped when emotion clogged his throat.

His parents had made a ton of sacrifices—all freely made, of course. But if Cooper could help them and make things easier, then that's exactly what he wanted to do.

Noel eyed him thoughtfully. "Your family sounds amazing. And your parents... I'd like to meet them someday." Her face turned a bright red as her eyes widened. "I just mean ... they sound inspirational ... I wasn't insinuating..."

Cooper chuckled. "You weren't insinuating I should take you home and introduce you to my family?" His words only made her look even more embarrassed. "I know what you meant, Noel. My parents were hoping to swing by on Saturday to see the store's progress. Depending on the time, you might be able to say hello to them then."

"That would be nice." Noel leaned over a piece of paper and seemed especially interested in writing the letters perfectly. Hair had fallen like a curtain, hiding her face from him.

On instinct, Cooper reached to sweep her hair back so he could see her face and stopped himself at the last second.

What was he thinking? He had no right to touch her hair. Yet, at the same moment, he realized that he was shocked by how much he wanted to.

The lights above reflected off the blonde tresses.

He cleared his throat, desperate for a different train of thought. "What about your parents? Do you just have the one sibling?"

"Jace. Yes, he's my only sibling. Older than me by two minutes."

"Twins. I'll bet that was interesting. Did you guys get along?"

"Best friends." She finally looked up and grinned, the earlier embarrassment seemingly forgotten. "We once knew another set of twins in middle school who couldn't stand each other. I couldn't even fathom how that was possible."

"That's really neat." There was a twelve-year difference between himself and Jett. As their parents said, Jett was an unexpected blessing. "I always thought it'd be nice to have a sibling close in age. What about your parents?"

The corners of Noel's mouth tugged down, and the smile that was there before disappeared. She hesitated, as though she were trying to decide how much to share.

NOEL HATED TALKING about her parents. For one thing, just thinking about them nudged her stress levels upward. But it was also difficult to explain what growing up was like because the moment someone heard she came from money, it was like everything changed.

How did she explain that she didn't have—or want—their money? Or that money wasn't everything?

But Cooper had stopped working on the sign, the words "Young Adult" only half written. He was watching her, curiosity obvious on his face.

"My parents have always been primarily uninvolved in our lives." Noel picked up a green pen and held it between her thumb and a finger. "My father is a successful business-man. Jace and I were raised by nannies while our parents went to business functions and traveled. During the summer, we were sent to live with our grandparents on my dad's side." She smiled as memories of the warm nights, cold swims, and endless laughter surfaced. "Jace and I used to imagine what it would be like to run away and just live there all the time." She glanced at Cooper, unsure what his response would be.

His brows rose in surprise. "Wow. I'm sure that was hard. Although your grandparents sound amazing."

"They were. They're both gone now, but Jace took over their sheep farm a couple of years ago. He, his wife, and their two boys live there now. I like to visit every chance I get."

"That's really neat. And what an amazing legacy to leave behind." Cooper sounded impressed. "It's too bad you can't live on the farm, too, since it meant so much to you."

Grandpa had willed it to both her and Jace. She still owned half of the ranch. She'd offered to sell Jace her half of it, but he refused. In fact, Jace had suggested she have a house built on the property and live there, too.

Noel kept thinking it might be something she'd do in the future. But for now, she liked being in town. Besides, what would she do on the farm? She didn't want to step on Bonnie's toes or crowd her brother's family. Even as she thought it, she knew they would never feel that way.

"Maybe I will someday." She shrugged, unwilling to go into the logistics of it all.

"Is your family local?"

"Yes. The farm is just outside Clearwater. My parents live here, too." Unfortunately. The way they talk about how amazing France is, Noel often wondered why they didn't just up and move there. "Conversations with my parents are usually kept to civil phone calls once a week. And a big Christmas party that they throw for all of their old friends and clients." She couldn't conceal the sarcasm dripping from her voice.

And Cooper clearly picked up on it immediately. "And I take it that you don't care for the party."

"It's mandatory to keep the peace." She set the pen down with the others. "But I dread it all year long."

"I'm sorry to hear that. Hopefully, you have other fun holiday gatherings that make up for it."

Noel latched onto the segue and thankfully changed the subject. "I've got a town-sized party to organize, and we need to get your store open so that it can be part of it." She smiled then and pointed to the list they were working on. "So tell me, what is your favorite book of all time?"

Cooper paused and looked up at the ceiling. "Oh, it's almost impossible to narrow it down to just one. Okay, how about this? One of my absolute favorites is *The Hobbit*. I remember we would sit in the living room in the evenings, and my mom would read a chapter or two aloud before it was time to go to bed." He smiled fondly, then went back to writing signs. "How about you? What's your favorite book?"

Without hesitation, Noel said, "*Anne of Green Gables*."

He chuckled. "No doubt, huh?"

"Nope. My grandma gave me a copy for my tenth birthday. I read that book so many times that it finally fell apart. I don't know what happened to it. I'm guessing my parents probably threw it out at some point." That part had always bothered her. She would have rather taped the copy and kept it forever if she could have.

"It's amazing how much of an impact a book can have on our lives, isn't it?"

"It sure is. And to think you can now play a small part in that for so many other people." Noel took a few extra seconds to look around the bookstore and take it all in.

There was still so much work to do, but the place exuded warmth and cheer. She had a feeling it would quickly become one of Clearwater's favorite businesses.

She studied Cooper's profile. A section of his dark hair had fallen over his forehead as he concentrated on writing the next sign. His eyelashes were so long that they nearly touched the lenses of his glasses. A neatly trimmed goatee covered his strong jaw.

Everything about the man spoke of kindness, strength, and determination—all traits she admired.

She was pretty sure Cooper and Jace would get along well, too.

Maybe, once the store was up and running, she'd invite Jace, Bonnie, and the kids to come take a look.

For reasons beyond what Noel was willing to examine right now, Jace's opinion of Cooper mattered a great deal.

5

A s soon as the perfectly seasoned brisket touched Cooper's tongue, he nodded his approval. It was lunchtime on Wednesday, and he'd decided to take a break from working on the bookstore.

He and Noel had stayed way too late the night before finishing the signs and then taping them around the store until they'd found a spot for every single category. The task had seemed horribly daunting at first, but between Noel's ability to slice tasks into smaller pieces, and the way they easily worked together, they got it done.

Today, he'd been slowly unpacking boxes and moving books to their assigned sections. Once that was done, he would then go through and alphabetize everything.

By the time ten thirty came around, his stomach was already growling. So he'd texted his mom to let her know he was bringing lunch and then swung through his favorite barbecue joint in town.

They were sitting around the square table in his parents' kitchen enjoying the meal.

"Thanks for bringing lunch by, son," Dad said as he lifted a forkful of roasted chicken.

"You're welcome. It sounded good today." Cooper motioned to Jett's plate. A reindeer plush—a recent favorite—sat next to it on the table. "Aren't you going to eat your macaroni and cheese?"

Over the years, Jett's appetite and favorite foods had varied greatly. But through it all, he'd always gravitated toward macaroni and cheese.

Jett shook his head. "Not today." But he stuffed a large bite of potato salad in his mouth.

"Okay, more for me." Cooper made an exaggerated move to steal his brother's macaroni.

"No!" Jett laughed hard as he covered the food with both hands. "Not for Cooper."

"I guess I'll let you keep it."

With humor shining in his eyes, Jett scooped up a bite of macaroni and ate it.

Mom chuckled. "So, how is the bookstore coming along?"

"Really well. There's been a lot of progress over the last couple of days."

"There's a nice lady," Jett announced, his food forgotten. "I can go with you to see the nice lady?" His attention was laser focused on Cooper.

Mom looked at him curiously.

Cooper laughed. "He's talking about Noel, the woman I hired to help get the bookstore organized and ready to open before Thanksgiving." He'd told his parents about her briefly yesterday when he dropped his brother off at home. "Jett has taken a real liking to her."

"She likes my reindeer." Jett jumped up from the table before any of them could stop him. When he returned, he had the same picture search book that he'd had with him on Monday night. He opened it and pointed to a reindeer. "She likes it."

The memory of seeing the two of them looking at the book brought a smile to Cooper's face. He wondered if Noel's interest in it was the reason why Jett now carried the reindeer plush around. "Noel was really good with him, too. She volunteers at Joyful Hope Stables. She knows the owners." He just couldn't remember what the connection was between them.

"I've heard a lot of great things about the stables," Dad said from the other side of the table.

They'd considered hippotherapy for Jett years ago, but Jett had a fear of horses that had spanned most of his life. They never could figure out what had sparked it.

Mom seemed to have forgotten her meal entirely. "How old is Noel? Is she single?"

Heat traveled up the back of Cooper's neck, and he fought to not react and cover it with a hand. "I have no idea how old she is." It was the truth, though he suspected they were close in age. "And as far as I can tell, she is single. But that hasn't really come up in conversation."

Cooper had to admit that while his parents had suggested many times that he needed to find someone and settle down with a family of his own, they'd never pushed him or made him feel pressured. Still, there was no missing that look of hope and interest in his mom's eyes. Or his dad's, either.

Given the nature of Jett's disability, Cooper was their only chance at having grandchildren. He did want kids of his own someday. Since Jett's disability was a genetic one, Cooper had gone to have his own DNA tested to see if he carried the gene for Fragile X. He did not.

Cooper had dated plenty over the years. And there had

been some women he'd been interested in. But most of the time, once they realized that Jett would eventually be living with them full time, the women had bowed out of the blossoming relationship.

He understood that. He even respected their decisions and their honesty.

And he'd been prepared for the idea of never finding a life partner. It'd be worth it because family was everything. He would never turn his back on Jett.

But still. Seeing how close his parents were and the kind of support they were for each other made Cooper wish he could find a love like that. A woman who was in it with him no matter what.

Was Noel that person? He certainly didn't know her well enough to even hazard a guess.

The fact that she'd warmed right up to Jett, and that his brother liked her, made Cooper want to get to know her better. Because if she was even half as nice as she seemed to be...

Entertaining possibilities like that was a distraction he didn't need right now. Especially with the imminent opening of the bookstore and the fact that the timing pretty much rested on Noel's ability to help keep things on track.

Thankfully, his parents didn't say anything more, even though he caught his mom looking at him curiously several times.

"How are you feeling, Mom?" Cooper studied her. The scar on her neck was healing nicely. The skin was still red along the incision, although the doctor assured her that would lessen over time, even though she'd always have a visible scar. He was thankful that she didn't seem to be self-conscious about it.

"I'm feeling well," she assured him with a smile. Dad

reached over and gave her hand a squeeze.

Jett shoveled the last of his macaroni and cheese into his mouth and grabbed his reindeer plush, which Dad had named Rudy, off the table. When he swallowed, he said, "I can go with Cooper to see the nice lady?"

"She's not going to be there until this evening, buddy. So how about you help Mom with all the chores, stay out of trouble, and I'll come get you at five? We'll take a sandwich and some chips over to the bookstore. Does that sound good?"

At first, it looked like Jett was going to argue about having to wait. But after thinking a moment, he gave a nod and left the kitchen.

Dad chuckled. "He sure looks forward to going to the bookstore with you."

"I'm glad." Cooper hoped that he could slowly teach Jett how to do some of the jobs there so that he and his brother could work together.

Cooper polished off the last of his lunch. "I'd probably better get back. It'd be nice if I made some decent progress before Noel comes in this evening." He stood and picked up his plate.

"Does she have somewhere to go for Thanksgiving?" The question came from Mom.

Cooper paused. "I know her brother and his family live in town. They seem close. I imagine they'll be spending the holiday together."

"You should check. There's always room for another chair at our table."

An outsider might see his mom's comment as being pushy. But all of Cooper's life, his parents had extra people over for the holidays. Sometimes, they were friends or neighbors, and sometimes, they were people his parents had just met. It wasn't out of character for Mom or Dad to suggest inviting someone over.

"I'll ask her about it tonight," he promised.

NOEL HAD BEEN surprised when she received a text from Cooper. They had exchanged numbers after she accepted the part-time position in case they needed to get a hold of each other.

Cooper's text said that he and Jett were bringing sandwiches and chips to the bookstore and that she was welcome to join them.

It sounded a lot better than eating something canned at home by herself. She swung by Clara's Café when she left work and picked up a dozen cookies, stopped at her house to change and pick up her car, then headed to the bookstore a little earlier than she had been going.

The building was open, and the brothers were already there when she arrived. She'd barely made it through the door before Jett was hurrying toward her, a plush reindeer clutched in his arms. He held it out to her. "Want to see my reindeer?"

"Of course." Noel set her messenger bag on the floor by her feet and reached her hands out. The animal was dark brown with lighter-colored antlers and a colorful red and green blanket over its back. "Oh, he is so soft and friendly. What's his name?"

"Rudy." Jett grinned as he took the plush back.

"Like Rudolph?"

Jett pointed to the deer's black nose. "He's not Rudolph," he said matter-of-factly.

A deep chuckle pulled Noel's attention from the younger Meyer brother to the older one. Cooper was unpacking food from a large plastic bag and placing it on the counter. He flashed her a smile that lifted her mood way more than it should have.

She picked her bag up again and walked in his direction. As she got closer, she caught a whiff of the food, and her stomach growled.

"That smells amazing." She got the cookies out and set them on the counter with everything else. "I didn't want to come empty-handed." She opened the small box to reveal the chocolate chip and frosting-covered sugar cookies.

"Thank you," he said as he gave the baked goods an appreciative look. "I didn't know what you liked, so I brought three kinds of sub sandwiches. We've got meatball marinara, turkey and Swiss, and chicken bacon ranch. What would you prefer?"

"Is there one that Jett likes the best?"

His gaze rested on her face briefly, and something flashed in his eyes that she couldn't quite read.

"I got him a plain ham and cheese. I like the other three, so whatever you don't eat, I'll choose from. Then I'll save the other for lunch tomorrow." He waved a hand over her choices.

"In that case, I'll take the turkey and Swiss, please." He handed the submarine sandwich to her, his fingers briefly brushing hers in the process. "Thank you."

"You're welcome." He chose the chicken bacon ranch and then put the third sandwich back in the bag. He handed her a bag of potato chips before turning to get Jett set up at the counter with his food.

There was little conversation for a few minutes as they all focused on their meals.

When Noel had a sandwich, she usually threw together basic ingredients from the fridge, and rarely did she have the veggies to put on it. She'd forgotten how much better a hot sandwich was, especially when the day was a bit chilly to start with. "This is really good. It was nice of you two to invite me to join you."

Cooper took a drink of his bottled water and cleared his throat. He pointed at her sandwich. "Speaking of turkey, are you getting together with your brother for Thanksgiving?"

With a shake of her head, Noel finished her bite and said, "Not this year. They're having Thanksgiving with Bonnie's family. She invited me to join them. I know her brother, but I don't really know the rest of her family that well. Especially considering I'd be flying and staying with them for a couple of days."

Besides, with the added stress of trying to get everything done before the Moonlight Stroll, it was probably just as well that she was local and free to tackle anything that came up.

"Well, if you're interested, my parents host a Thanksgiving lunch. You're welcome to join us."

Noel was so surprised by his words that it took a moment for them to sink in. He was inviting her to his parents' house for Thanksgiving? Her confusion and surprise must have been evident on her face because he set his sandwich down with a chuckle.

"Sorry, I should've given you a frame of reference. My parents host a Thanksgiving lunch, and every year, they invite a few people who are either alone for the holiday or just don't have anywhere to eat a traditional Thanksgiving dinner."

Jett looked up from his book. "I hate turkey."

Cooper covered his mouth with one hand while he clearly fought back a smile. "We don't say we hate a food, buddy. Remember? You can just say, 'No, thank you' when someone offers it and then eat something else that's available."

"No thank you for turkey."

"All right. That's better." Cooper shook his head, his eyes glittering with amusement. "Anyway, they've invited a neighbor who isn't going to see her kids this year and someone Dad worked with for years. My mom mentioned I should check with you to see if you had any plans."

So the invitation had come from his mom, not Cooper himself. Noel was surprised by the mixed emotions that realization brought up. Because, when he first invited her, there'd been a small thrill thinking that he wanted to spend Thanksgiving with her, or at least spend time outside of the bookstore together.

But then, shortly after that, came the doubt and anxiety. Why was he inviting her? If he brought her for Thanksgiving, would his parents get the wrong idea?

Now that she knew his parents hosted people for Thanksgiving and that his mom had suggested the invitation, there was relief followed by an unexpected pang of disappointment.

Disappointment that it wasn't Cooper himself who had wanted to ask her.

Which was completely ridiculous. She was here to help him get the store ready. He was even paying her. The fact that he invited her to join him and Jett for sandwiches meant little to nothing.

She stepped over her pride, which had taken a face-plant, and dabbed at her mouth with a napkin. "I appreciate that. And please tell your mom as much. But I'm probably going to just grab something quick. I'll need to be on hand to make sure the event that night is all prepared."

Cooper gave her a doubtful look. "I get it, trust me. I'll be here making sure everything is ready for our official opening. But I'm still planning to take time to eat a Thanksgiving meal. I mean, you have to eat, right? And it's lunch.

There's plenty of time to whip everyone into shape afterward."

He wasn't wrong. Still, the whole thing seemed awkward.

"Tell you what," he began as he jotted something down on a piece of paper. "Here's their address. It's still over a week away. If you decide on Thanksgiving that you want a traditional dinner with friends, stop by. You don't even have to RSVP."

He handed it to her then. She glanced at it and slipped it into her pocket. "Thank you. I appreciate the invitation."

With a single nod, Cooper focused on finishing his sandwich, and Noel did the same and took note of the bookstore. Cooper had made a lot of progress throughout the day, and the difference was noticeable.

"It's looking good in here."

He seemed pleased by her comment. "It's coming along, isn't it? Even if I can't put some of the little details in place before opening, I can make sure it's all set up before the Christmas event."

"Definitely. As long as people can come in, get an idea of what your store has to offer, and buy books, you'll be up and running for next week. Bonus points if you put up lights or decorations outside."

"Oh, I'm definitely going to have lights in the windows. Next year, I'll hire someone to come and paint some scenes on the panes." He started picking trash up off the counter and tossing it into a bag. "You'd mentioned at one point that the town usually has a few decorations that are set out as well?"

"Yes. This year's theme is oversized toys, so we'll have decorations to put out with the hot chocolate and cookie stations and to loan to any other businesses that aren't wanting to decorate their stores." She'd taken pictures of the toy soldiers to Mr. Brooks to see if that would help persuade him to let her decorate the outside of his business. It made no difference.

Cooper was watching her. "Is that something you have a problem with? Getting businesses to participate?"

"There is one in particular. One of my co-workers is much better at the whole public relations thing than I am. But she had to head out of town for a family emergency, and her job landed on my lap this year."

"And someone has been giving you trouble about decorating. Like just not wanting to participate or being rude?"

He straightened his back a little as he asked the question, and even though he was likely simply curious, it was almost like he was concerned.

"Well, this gentleman is on the older side. He has been pretty rude, but that's not unusual. Elsie—that's my co-worker —tends to have more of a way of reaching him. Me? Not so much."

"I can put up twice the decorations if that helps," Cooper told her with a wink.

It was a little thing. A joking gesture. And it warmed Noel's heart.

"You're very kind, sir," she said with a sweep of her hand. "But it'll all be okay. Now, what do you say we get back to stocking these shelves?"

Jett jumped up from his seat, excitement on his face. He started to reach for Noel's hand but stopped himself before crossing his arms in front of him. "This one. Let's fix this one." He led the way to a bookshelf in the children's section of the store. Halfway there, he ran back to the counter to grab Rudy before returning.

A thought popped into Noel's head. "You know, we have a group that comes in with a couple of live reindeer for A Country Christmas. Maybe Jett would enjoy seeing them?"

Cooper frowned, a tinge of sadness on his face. "In theory? He would love it. But we normally steer clear of the event because it's too much for Jett. There are too many people, it's loud, and he's scared of horses. The horse-drawn carriage is a constant worry for him as we walk around downtown."

Noel watched as Jett sat on a bean bag chair that Cooper must have brought into the store today. The younger man held Rudy on his lap while he read a book about Santa and his reindeer.

It was a shame that Jett couldn't meet real reindeer. But now that Cooper pointed it out, Noel realized he was right. She could barely handle the crowds during A Country Christmas herself, and she was paid to be out there making sure everything was coming together smoothly.

Maybe they needed to figure out a way to incorporate an activity or two for those in their community who struggled with the crowd.

As she and Cooper started working on the bookshelves, Noel's mind was rushing through a list of possibilities. She decided that she would reach out to Wyatt and see if he had any suggestions.

6
_____

Over the course of the week, the time in the evenings that Cooper spent working with Noel seemed to go quickly. Not only were they getting the bookstore put together beautifully, but it was happening way faster than he'd ever imagined.

It wasn't just because she was actually helping him move the books, but it was also because of her ability to map everything out. It made it easier for him to work during the day and accomplish a lot before she arrived later.

The neat thing about it was that she was always very positive about the progress and jumped right into the middle of wherever he'd left off.

Now, it was Saturday morning. Jett was at home with their parents, and Cooper was waiting at the bookstore for Noel.

Truthfully, he could probably finish getting the last of the books onto the shelves himself, but Noel insisted on coming in by nine so she could help. He wasn't going to argue with her because he much preferred her company to working alone.

Cooper had several more decorations coming in over the next few days, so he took the time to check those shipping notices while he waited for Noel to arrive.

When the door opened and the chimes rang out, he couldn't stop the smile that came to his face.

Noel walked in with a smile of her own that seemed to brighten the entire room. She wore a pair of sneakers, blue jeans, and a red sweater with stitched snowflakes all over the front. She'd pulled her blonde hair into a ponytail that hung high on the back of her head. It swung back and forth as she crossed the room toward him.

"Good morning," she greeted as she lifted a paper bag. "I brought scones." Her brows drew together. "I guess I should have asked first. Do you like scones?"

"What's not to like?"

His comment immediately erased the lines between her eyebrows. The smile returned as she unpacked the bag. "I brought cinnamon and chocolate chip. I like both, so you pick your favorite."

That was no contest. He reached for the chocolate chip, and her smile brightened.

"I like both as well, but cinnamon is my favorite. For the record, if cinnamon is a flavor option for anything, then that'll be my first choice." She bit into the scone, and her eyes closed briefly as she enjoyed the pastry. "Clara makes the best scones, especially if you can get them in the morning right after she bakes them."

Noel had nearly finished her bite before Cooper realized he had been staring. He cleared his throat, focused on the to-do list she'd pulled out of her bag, and started on his own scone.

They went over their game plan while they ate breakfast and then got to work organizing the books on the last bookcase. Two hours later, everything was in order, and the final boxes had been broken down and added to the stack in the alley behind the store.

It was all finally coming together. The store was still devoid of posters, pictures, and the other items he wanted to add. But he wouldn't hesitate to let a potential customer through the door now.

And it was all thanks to the woman standing beside him.

"I think everyone's going to love it," she said softly. "This is a great place, Cooper."

"I'm pretty happy with it. And I wouldn't have made it this far without your help." Before he allowed himself to think about it, he put an arm around her shoulders and gave her one of those side friend hugs that he'd given to many other people in the past.

Except this time, the moment she was nestled against his side, the last thing he wanted to do was let her go. For such a simple gesture, it didn't feel as friendly as he'd intended it to. He dropped his arm immediately, afraid that his thoughts might come through his actions. He turned to face her.

"Seriously, Noel, thank you."

"You're welcome." She smiled at him then. "So come on, there has to be something else we can do. Didn't you say the posters came in yesterday?"

"They did," he replied slowly. "But between your day job and helping me here, you've been working nonstop. Seriously, I've monopolized a lot of your time lately. Don't you have somewhere else you had to go this afternoon?"

"I do. I'm helping Wyatt at Joyful Hope. They're having a cookie decorating event there for any special needs families in town that would like to go." She paused. "I thought maybe you and Jett would like to check it out."

Cooper didn't know what he expected her to say, but that

certainly wasn't it. Was she hoping they would stop by? Or was she asking them to go with her? A small difference, really, but it mattered.

Finally, reality crowded in. "Jett is petrified of horses. Seriously, Noel, he freaks out."

She held up a hand to stop him. "Joyful Hope isn't all about horses. I mean, that's the way they started. But they have an amazing center that they use for classes and things like that. This afternoon, everything will be inside. Jett won't even have to see a horse."

Having another outlet for Jett would be good. Besides, he and their parents had been talking about trying to do more holiday-related activities this year. Decorating cookies might be perfect.

And it would be interesting to see Noel in a different setting, too.

"My parents are going to bring Jett by later to see how the store is coming along. I'll talk to Jett then. If he wants to go, we'll be there."

Noel's smile brightened. "Okay. Good." She ran both hands over her head to smooth her hair and tightened the ponytail. Some strands had fallen loose, though, and hung next to the side of her face.

It took everything Cooper had not to reach out and tuck them behind her ear.

NOEL HELPED Cooper hang posters and pictures around the bookstore. Having the bright images added a lot to the place —especially the children's section.

She smiled up at the large poster depicting the cover of

Charlotte's Web. Another poster had a large, green dragon on it with wings spread as it soared over a town.

They found book stands and chose a wide range of the newest or most popular books to set out on top of the book-shelves to hopefully snag the kids' attention. Between that and the beanbag chair on the floor, it was enough to make Noel want to choose a book and read for a while herself.

One of those books on display was a story about reindeer that Cooper said he bought before Jett had become interested in the animal.

"Your brother is going to be so excited when he sees that book," Noel said with a smile on her face.

Cooper nodded knowingly. "I have a feeling he'll be leaving the store with it." He slipped his hands in his pockets. "It's really coming together. I made a sign last night to put on the door, letting people know it will be open for the first time on Thanksgiving evening. Today, I'm finally feeling confident enough to display it."

"That's wonderful, Cooper. You should definitely put it up."

She watched as he retrieved the sign from behind the counter along with a suction cup to hang it on the glass door.

As he put it in place, she noticed that one of the pictures they'd hung up was slightly crooked. She moved the step stool over to the science fiction section and stood on it so that she could reach the framed image.

It didn't take much to straighten it. Satisfied, she started to step down and got the edge of her shoe caught on the side of the stool.

Noel felt herself shift off balance. One moment, she was certain she was going to fall. The next, a large hand gripped her arm to steady her.

"Whoa. Are you okay?" Cooper helped her to the floor

and made sure she was steady. He leaned in to look at her face. "That was close."

"Yeah. I'm fine. Thank you." She swallowed hard. Her pulse raced, but she wasn't sure how much of that was thanks to the near fall or because he still had one hand resting against her lower back.

Between the panic attack when she first met him and now nearly falling on her rear... "I promise I'm usually quite capable of using a step stool without nearly breaking an arm."

"I have no doubt."

He studied her face for a moment, his hand warm even through the fabric of her sweater. Something shifted in his gaze.

But before Noel even had a chance to figure out what it meant, the bookstore door opened, accompanied by the chimes.

Cooper's hand dropped as he turned to greet Jett along with an older couple who had to be his parents. Even if she hadn't known they were coming, there was no missing the similarities between father and sons.

Jett hurried to Noel, Rudy tucked under one arm and a big smile on his face. "I knew you would be here." He lifted the toy. "I brought Rudy." He held it out to her.

Noel accepted the toy and gave it a hug. "Well, it's good to see you, Jett. And you, too, Rudy."

Jett took the reindeer back, looking pleased. Only then did he take a look around the store. His mouth opened when he saw the children's area. "Whoa!"

Watching his brother's reaction brought a smile to Cooper's face. "Noel, these are my parents, David and Rachel. Guys, this is Noel. She's pretty much a miracle worker. Trust me, we'd be tripping over boxes right now if it weren't for her."

Mr. Meyer shook her hand, and Mrs. Meyer gave her a friendly smile.

"It's wonderful to meet you," Mrs. Meyer told her. "Jett has spoken a great deal about you."

Noel could feel the heat in her face at the idea that she had come up in conversation at the Meyer household. "Well, Jett is a sweet guy."

"Look! Cooper, look!" Jett approached them with the reindeer book in his hands. "It's about Rudy."

Cooper put an arm around his little brother's shoulders. "Why don't you take it over to the bean bag chair and look through it? See if it's any good."

"Okay." Without hesitation, he settled in to look through his new find.

Mr. Meyer took in the store and nodded his approval. "It looks real nice, Coop." He clapped his oldest son on the shoulder. "I'm proud of you."

"For everything," Mrs. Meyer added with a head tilt toward Jett. She gave Cooper a hug.

Noel suddenly felt like she was intruding on a special family moment. She walked over to the main counter to give them a little more space. Besides, she probably needed to get out of there and over to the stables to help Wyatt and his wife, Chrissy, set up for the event.

She was retrieving her bag when Cooper approached. "You heading out?"

"I should. I know they can use some help setting up for the cookie decorating."

"Hold on a minute," he said as he briefly touched her arm. He turned and called out to his brother. "Jett. Do you want to go decorate Christmas cookies this afternoon?"

Jett seemed to think it over for a moment. Finally, he nodded. "To eat the cookies."

"Yes, I'm sure you'll get to eat the cookie you decorate."

Jett seemed satisfied with that.

Cooper explained the event to his parents. "I can take Jett over for that before bringing him back to the house."

"Do you think he'll go in since it's at the stables?" Mrs. Meyer asked, clearly uncertain.

Noel stepped forward. "There's a large learning center there. You have to go through it to get to the stables. Jett won't even see a horse."

Cooper nodded. "I'll text you and let you know if we get there and Jett refuses to go inside. That way, you don't think we just changed our minds if we don't show up."

"Sounds like fun." Noel shouldered her bag. "It was nice to meet you both," she told Mr. and Mrs. Meyer. She raised a hand and waved. "Bye, Jett. Have fun with the book."

"Bye!" he said as he waved back.

With a last look in Cooper's direction, Noel left the family behind. As she walked back to her house, her phone pinged with a text.

"Hopefully I'll see you in about an hour."

Unable to keep a smile from her face, she texted back a response.

"I'm looking forward to it."

7

Noel had barely arrived at Joyful Hope before she was put to work, taking sprinkles and candies to each station so that visitors could easily reach a variety. Once she finished with that, she distributed plain sugar cookies at each of the five tables before choosing one to manage.

A sixth table was set up for those who were limited to gluten-free choices. Obviously, they couldn't cater to every single allergy. But gluten allergies were common and something they could provide an alternative to.

The cookie-decorating event was set to last an hour and a half. There was already a small crowd waiting when Chrissy, Wyatt's wife, opened the doors. She balanced their adorable son, one-year-old Zachary, on one hip.

She smiled as she greeted each person as they came through the door, and Zachary happily waved his chubby little hand.

Noel stood on her tiptoes to see if Cooper and Jett were among the group coming in. When she didn't see them, she squelched a pang of disappointment.

There was no time to dwell on it, though. Not when several young children were headed her way with smiles on their faces and eyes glued to the treats waiting for them.

Some of the children required little to no help. There were others that had a difficult time spreading frosting or adding candy.

Noel was more than happy to assist however she could.

Many of the kids took giant bites of their cookies as soon as they were finished. Small bottles of water and tables waited so that everyone could finish their treats. Bags were provided if they wanted to take the cookies home.

It was forty minutes into the event when Noel heard a deep voice say, "Hi, Noel." She knew immediately who it belonged to.

She looked up to find Cooper smiling at her. He seemed genuinely happy to see her, but there was a harried look on his face.

There was no chance to ask if everything was okay. Jett skirted around the table to stand next to Noel. His attention kept darting around the room until it finally settled on her.

"Don't like horses."

"It took half an hour to talk him into coming inside," Cooper said. "I'm convinced the only reason why he did was because he knew you were here."

"Horses are scary." Jett kept his elbows tucked into his sides and his hands clasped in front of him.

A little girl needed help using a spoon to sprinkle chocolate chips onto her cookie. When she'd finished and moved further down the table, Noel turned back to Jett, who hadn't left her side.

"Do you want to decorate a cookie?"

Jett kept looking around the room as though he was sure a

horse was going to come running in at any minute. He shook his head.

Cooper frowned, a worried look on his face. "Maybe it's better if we go."

Noel hated for them to leave. Not everyone who came to Joyful Hope was excited or even relaxed at first. She'd heard plenty of stories from Wyatt and Chrissy about kids, especially, who feared horses and grew to love them and connect with them over time.

With Jett's trepidation, she didn't want to introduce him to a horse. But getting him to feel comfortable in the learning center at the stables would be a big first step toward overcoming that fear in the future.

"Jett." She waited a moment for him to look at her. "Did you see all of the sprinkles and frosting that we have to put on cookies?" He nodded. "I've been trying to help the kids decorate their cookies, but I could use some help. Do you think you could be my helper today?"

Jett's eyes lit up. "I can help Noel."

"That would be great. Here, let's get you a pair of gloves. We wear these to help keep the cookies and sprinkles clean." She helped him pull clear gloves on his hands. "Now why don't you pick two kinds of candy or sprinkles to help with."

The younger man pointed to M&M'S and then a bowl of brightly colored sprinkles that included green trees and red Santa hats.

"Those are great choices. Okay, if a little boy or girl comes up and needs help, then you can be their helper."

Jett stood a little straighter. Now, instead of scanning the room for horses, he was watching the door as more children came into the room. Several of them headed their way.

Cooper came around the end of the table and gently

cupped her elbow with his hand. When he spoke, he was close enough for her to feel his breath against her cheek.

"You are amazing with him. Do you need any more help?"

"How are you with frosting?" She turned her head to look at him, surprised by how close he was standing.

"I can hold my own." His gaze dropped to her mouth for a heartbeat before returning to her eyes.

"Then, by all means." She waved toward the other end of the table.

Once he'd passed by her, the air that touched her face suddenly seemed chilly. She couldn't shake the way he'd looked at her. Surely, it was just their close proximity and her overactive imagination. But for a half second there, she'd thought he might want to kiss her.

She glanced at him. He was helping Jett with something as a family approached the table. Noel shook her head and tried to ignore the ridiculous thoughts trying to take up residence in her mind.

For the rest of the event, the three of them managed the table and helped a dozen more kids decorate their cookies. Jett seemed to enjoy being able to help others and didn't seem to mind if either Noel or Cooper had to give him some additional assistance.

When the last of their little decorators had left, the entire table was a mess. All of the toppings that Noel had painstakingly separated were mixed together.

She gently nudged Jett's arm. "Hey, look at that. There are three cookies left. Do you want to decorate them and take them home to your mom and dad?"

Now that there wasn't a crowd and all fear of horses had been forgotten, Jett quickly rounded the table and began to work on his own treats.

Cooper watched as his younger brother began to spread frosting on top of the cookies. "I have no idea what kind of a turnout you guys usually get here, but that seemed to be a success."

"Most definitely." Judging from the other tables, they'd had enough cookies, but not by many.

Wyatt walked across the room and held out a hand to Cooper. "I saw you jump in and help. I appreciate it. I'm Wyatt Tabor."

"Cooper Meyer."

The men shook hands.

Wyatt took in the frosting and sprinkle disaster that was their table. "We had a much higher attendance than we anticipated and not nearly enough people working tables." He smiled at Noel. "I'm really glad you volunteered. We'll remember to try to have more people available for our next event."

Noel tried to brush sprinkles into a bowl and gave up. "Are you kidding? It was so much fun." She looked down and realized that there was chocolate frosting on the front of her shirt and laughed.

Wyatt joined her. "You may be taking ingredients home one way or another." He turned to Jett. "And who are you?"

Jett looked at Cooper first, then back at Wyatt. "My name is Jett."

"Well, it's nice to meet you. Thank you for helping the kids."

"You're welcome. Now I am making cookies." Jett added a generous amount of chocolate sprinkles to his first cookie.

"I'm happy to see that," Wyatt told him.

"Jett is Cooper's brother," Noel told him. "I'd invited them to come so Jett could decorate some cookies, but he was more interested in helping at first."

Wyatt jogged to a small table against one wall and brought a flyer back. "We have two more activities scheduled between now and Christmas." He handed it to Cooper. "Jett is welcome to come by for either of them."

"I appreciate that."

"All right, I'd better go check on Chrissy. I've heard rumors she's cleaning up after a frosting explosion, and I'm willing to bet our son is in need of a nap soon."

"Oh no! Does she need more help?"

Wyatt held up a hand. "You've been a huge help already between setting up and manning the tables. You should head out. We appreciate you, Noel." He shook Cooper's hand again. "It was nice meeting you. I hope to see you and Jett again soon."

With that, he took his leave.

"He seems nice," Cooper said. "Remind me what connection he has to you."

Noel chuckled. "He's my brother's wife's brother. How's that for being clear as mud?"

"Well, he's got a really neat place here."

"Cooper." Jett held up his hands, both of which had icing on them. "I'm all done."

Noel pointed to the restrooms. "Why don't you clean up, and I'll put your cookies on a plate so you can take them home?"

Noel watched as Cooper led Jett to the restrooms.

It had been so much fun to have them there volunteering with her.

She'd enjoyed working with Cooper in general over the last week. She'd be sorry to see the job end after Tuesday. It hadn't taken long to get used to seeing him every day.

The thought saddened her.

When Cooper and Jett returned, she had the cookies ready

to go. Jett was looking tired and a little anxious. She handed the plate to him. "Here you go. I hope your dad and mom like them. You did a great job decorating them."

"Thank you," Jett said. "You go to the bookstore tomorrow?"

"No. Tomorrow's Sunday, and I have church with my family. But maybe I'll see you there on Monday." She cut a glance at Cooper, hoping she hadn't spoken out of turn.

Jett looked disappointed but started to lead the way toward the main door.

"I'd better catch up to him. Thanks for suggesting this. It was fun." Jett was halfway across the room. Cooper turned and started jogging after him. He looked over his shoulder and gave a small wave before they disappeared through the door.

BY THE TIME Cooper got to his apartment late that night, he was exhausted. After decorating cookies, he'd taken Jett back home to find Mom had made stew and cornbread. He stayed for dinner and then headed home.

He put the leftovers his mom had given him in the fridge then sank into the comfort of his recliner. He thought back over the day, and a smile tugged at the corners of his mouth.

Spending time with Noel—both at the bookstore this morning and at the cookie decorating event—had made his day. She was easy to be around, and there was something about her that made the time fly by.

She had a lot on her plate, with the Moonlight Stroll only a few days away. But when that was over, he was seriously considering asking her out to lunch or dinner.

He pulled his phone out and went to his contacts list.

Noel's name stood out. Before letting himself think twice, he started a text to her and sent it.

"Are you as tired as I am?"

A minute later, a response came in.

"Definitely. Did you have a good rest of your evening?"

"It was fine. I just got home."

He wanted to ask if she ended up helping clean everything up at the stables after all, but suddenly all the texting seemed like a lot.

"Is it okay if I call you?"

He waited for several moments, wondering if he'd overstepped, when the answer popped up.

"Sure."

Cooper couldn't have stopped the smile on his face if he tried. He dialed her number and waited for her to answer.

"Hello again."

The soft tone of her voice came through the phone and settled over him like a comforting hug.

"Hey. Did you make it out of the stables without drowning in frosting?"

She laughed. "Yes, but I did go back and help Chrissy clean up the mess before I left."

Cooper wasn't the least bit surprised about that. "Jett had a lot of fun. Helping others like he did was good for him. He was really proud of the cookies when he gave them to our parents."

"I'm glad to hear that."

He'd looked at the flyer Wyatt had given them. The other events were during the day, and Cooper didn't think he'd be able to take Jett. But he definitely wanted to check out the events that were regularly scheduled after the new year.

"Do you know if Wyatt would be open to Jett helping out at some events after the new year? I'll be right there with him. It's hard because he's got the body of a twenty-six-year-old, but his emotional age is more like that of a six-year-old. Then, his intellectual age is something else entirely. I think being able to help the younger kids makes him feel older and more mature. If that even makes sense."

Cooper cringed. Here, he had Noel on the phone—a beautiful woman he was definitely attracted to—and all he was talking about was his brother. No wonder he wasn't married yet.

But what about Noel? She seemed to be single, and from what he knew about her, he couldn't possibly understand why.

"That makes complete sense. Let me talk to Wyatt and get the official okay, but I don't see why that would be a problem." She paused. "I'm trying to see if we can set up something like a toned-down version of A Clearwater Christmas for families with special needs. One where people like Jett can see the reindeer or visit with Santa without all the noise and crowds."

It took several moments to digest her words. She had a crazy busy schedule with work and now helping him open the bookstore. Even through that, she was going to take the extra time to organize something for Jett and others like him.

Cooper was stunned by her thoughtfulness.

"If you don't think that's a good idea, just tell me." Her tone sounded uncertain.

"Sorry, Noel. My silence wasn't because I didn't think your idea was a good one. Just the opposite. I've been blown away by your kindness towards Jett. Thank you." If they were in the same room right now, he would've drawn her into a hug.

"You're welcome."

Neither of them spoke, and Cooper was afraid she was going to end the conversation. "It's going to seem weird not seeing you tomorrow."

"I was thinking the same thing."

"I don't suppose you've changed your mind about having Thanksgiving lunch at my parents' house, have you?"

"Honestly? I feel a little awkward just showing up at their house when I've only seen them once. I really don't want to intrude."

The uncertainty in her voice was difficult to miss, even over the phone.

"What if you came as my guest instead?" He held his breath and wished he could see her expression right now.

"Cooper..."

"I'd really like to keep seeing you even after you're not working at the store anymore."

"I would like that, too."

He smiled with relief. It wasn't like he'd asked her out or anything, but it was a good first step. "Awesome. So, tell me about this frosting explosion..."

8

Noel held her arms out and waited for Bonnie to transfer baby Grayson. Noel cuddled the drowsy four-month-old close and breathed in his wonderful scent. She saw her brother's family at least once a week, often more than that, and she never tired of spending time with her nephews.

"Auntie!" Gunner ran across the church foyer to wrap his little arms around Noel's legs.

She shifted Grayson to one arm and bent down so she could give her oldest nephew the squeeze hug he deserved. "Hey, kiddo. You been good this week?"

Gunner shrugged as though he had no idea, but it was what it was. Noel laughed. "That's what I thought. What was your favorite thing this last week?"

"I got to help Daddy get the Christmas decorations out of the barn. I even got to push the dolly!"

"Wow! That's amazing. You must be strong. Let me see those muscles."

Gunner flexed his arms and scrunched his face with the exaggerated motion. Noel struggled not to chuckle. Instead, she felt the muscle in his arm appreciatively. "I'm sure glad you were able to be such a big help."

Jace walked up then and placed a hand on the back of his son's neck. "We wanted to go ahead and get all the decorations down so we can put the tree up as soon as we get back from our Thanksgiving trip."

"I can't WAIT!" Gunner jumped high into the air and landed back on his feet.

With a tender smile on her face, Bonnie reached for his hand. While she wasn't technically his biological mother, she'd been his nanny for nearly his whole life. Then, once Jace and Bonnie married, it all became official.

"Come on, buddy, let's get you to your class."

Noel continued to hold Grayson close. The little boy was sleeping soundly now, completely unaware of the church noises around him.

Jace put an arm around her shoulders to give her a hug. "Bonnie has soup on at the house. We thought we might just go back there for lunch if you don't mind. Otherwise, if you need to get back early, we can eat in town somewhere."

"No, soup at the house sounds great." She hadn't seen Jace or his family much over the last couple of weeks. As far as she was concerned, the entire Sunday was set aside for church and for them.

"Great!" Jace grinned at her as they headed into the sanctuary together.

Three hours later, they were all seated around the large table at the ranch and enjoying bowls of loaded baked potato soup. Gunner had tried the soup but was eating a grilled cheese sandwich instead.

Bonnie had already fed Grayson once they got to the house. Now, the baby was resting in Noel's arms again.

Truthfully, she loved holding the little boy. But she also

knew it gave Jace and Bonnie a chance to eat with both hands, something they didn't get to experience very often in the last few months.

"I still wish you were coming with us for Thanksgiving," Jace said before scooping up another spoonful of soup.

Noel shook her head. "I'm fine. Truly. Besides, if I'm feeling like I'm deprived of a Thanksgiving meal, I've been invited to a lunch on Thursday." She and Cooper hadn't exactly solidified those plans. He'd offered for her to go with him as a guest. She still didn't know if he was asking her like a date or just as a friend. The conversation had moved past their mutual admission of hoping to see each other even after the store was opened and centered on friendly conversation until they'd hung up the phone.

Bonnie's eyes lit up. "That's great! You should go. Seriously."

"Who invited you?"

Sweet Jace. Always looking out for her.

"Cooper. The owner of the bookstore I've been helping with. His parents have a big lunch every year and invite anyone who isn't going somewhere else for Thanksgiving." She tried to keep her response casual. Noel wasn't sure what was going on between her and Cooper—if anything at all— and didn't feel like having that come up in conversation.

Curiosity flashed in Jace's eyes. "That's really nice of them." He gave her a knowing smile. "Well, we'll be flying out first thing Wednesday morning and getting back on Satur- day." He glanced at Bonnie.

"I'll send you the itineraries," she confirmed.

"Thank you." Grayson waved a little fist in the air, and then reached for a section of Noel's hair. She freed it from his grasp and kissed his chubby hand. "I'm going to miss you, little guy."

"What about me, Auntie?" The question came from Gunner. He'd stacked the crusts from his grilled cheese sandwich on his plate and was slowly tipping the plate to see how far he could go before they fell. He looked up at Noel, his little innocent face in a pout. "Are you gonna miss me, too?"

"Are you kidding? I'm going to miss you sooooo much!" She spread her arms as wide as she could with a baby on her lap. "I can't wait to hear all about your adventures."

AFTER ONLY SPEAKING with Noel through text a time or two on Sunday and waiting all day Monday, Cooper was more than ready to see her when she walked through the bookstore entrance that evening.

Even though she flashed him a smile, there was a shadow of stress and worry in her eyes. She set her stuff on the floor by the main counter and barely turned in time to see Jett coming in for a hug.

Normally, he would've reprimanded Jett for hugging someone he didn't know. Except that wasn't true anymore.

And the sincere way she hugged him back illustrated that she felt the same way.

Cooper just wished he had permission to embrace her right now as well, especially when she looked like she could use it.

"Is everything okay?"

Jett was showing her pictures of reindeer he'd found in a dictionary. Noel spent the time commenting on the pictures and admiring them until Jett went to sit down with his book. She turned to Cooper.

"You remember me telling you about my co-worker,

Elsie, the one who had to leave at the last minute to care for her family?"

"The reason why you're having to do so much for the Christmas events this year."

"Exactly. Well, she called in this morning to let us know that she's going to come back in January to sell her house and then move to be closer to family permanently." She paused and took in several deep breaths. "My boss is hoping to roll my job and Elsie's into one and have me take over." She shook her head and swallowed several times. Her face looked flushed.

Cooper remembered her panic attack the first time he saw her and directed her to a chair. "Hey. You're okay here. Take a few minutes to breathe and relax."

She nodded and cradled her head in her hands, her elbows resting on the counter.

With slow, repetitive motion, Cooper rubbed her upper back with one hand and said nothing. Instead, he prayed silently. *Father, please help her to let some of this go. Bring her some of Your peace and strength.*

Noel's breathing slowed a little, and her shoulders, which were bunched and tight, started to relax.

She finally dropped her arms and raised her head.

Cooper took his cue and stopped rubbing her back. He took a seat in the chair next to her and swiveled to face her.

"You don't want the job," he said simply.

"I want my job. I don't want Elsie's." She waved her hand at the door leading out onto the square. "I can't even get Mr. Brooks to put up Christmas decorations. I'm not a people person. I don't belong in any form of public relations job. And honestly, my boss, Arlene, knows it. I could see it in her face when she told me."

"So you'll find another job. Something that suits you

better. Something closer to what you were doing before this whole mess with your co-worker." He directed her attention to the bookstore that was nearly ready to open. A feat he never would've imagined possible last week. "Look at what you accomplished here. Maybe you can open your own business organizing other people's lives or helping companies get their stock or stores under control."

"In theory, that sounds good. But as a business owner, that means I have to be the one to communicate with everyone. And that's not in my skill set."

Cooper reached over and covered one of her hands with his. "You are selling yourself short. Look at what you did here. And you communicated everything just fine with me."

"You are different." As soon as the words left her lips, her cheeks warmed.

"Different, how?" He looked down at their hands and lightly ran the pad of one finger up and down the back of her thumb.

She followed the movement with her eyes for a moment, then raised her chin. "I get nervous around most people that I don't know well. I never felt that way around you." Her voice was soft, the words quiet but sincere.

Cooper released a slow breath, then took her hand in his. He'd just worked up the courage to tell her he felt as though they'd known each other for a lot longer than a week when the bookstore's door opened. The chime sounded as a woman entered.

Noel turned her head to look and immediately jumped to her feet. Her hand slipped from his, and her face paled.

The woman took one glance at Noel, and the frown on her face deepened. "That unpleasant woman at your office said you might be here. As if it weren't bad enough before, now you're going to demean yourself further by working in a place like this?" She looked around the building as though she'd walked into a seedy bar instead of a bookstore.

Noel's spine straightened, and she crossed her arms in front of her. "Mother, there is nothing wrong with working in a bookstore. There was no need for you to come here—you should have called me."

"To have you ignore me. Again."

Noel didn't deny the accusation. "I planned to call you this evening once I got off work."

The older woman held her arms wide. "Then I've saved you the trouble." For the first time, she spared Cooper a glance. "And who might this be?"

Noel half turned toward him. "This is Cooper Meyer. He's the owner of this store that'll be opening in a few days. Cooper, this is my mother, Leslie Echolls."

Cooper gave what he hoped was a friendly nod. "It's good to meet you." It was a lie, but if he said how he really felt, it would be rude. That anyone would come in and make Noel feel as uncomfortable as she clearly did just now was beyond him. He wanted to ask her to leave but decided it would be best to take his cues from Noel.

He glanced over at Jett, relieved that his brother was busy in the children's corner and didn't seem to be paying them any attention.

Mrs. Echolls seemed to size Cooper up, found him lacking, and then turned her attention back to Noel. "I informed you last week that I needed the name for your plus one. Otherwise, I will arrange for your escort tomorrow. I have several names of young men who I know will be happy to step in."

There was no missing the way Noel's jaw clenched or how her eyes flashed.

What was going on here? A plus one for what? Was this

for the Christmas party Noel had told him about? Where on earth did Mrs. Echolls come off thinking she could just arrange someone for Noel? He felt like he was waiting for a punchline that never came.

The instinct to protect Noel was so strong that he had to plunge his hands into his pockets and take a deep, calming breath.

Noel spoke then, her voice on edge. "If you'd waited for me to call you this evening, I would have told you..."

Cooper stepped forward and put an arm around her shoulders. "...That she had a plus one. Me. So there'll be no need to arrange anything."

The way that Mrs. Echolls' eyes widened to the size of saucers told Cooper that that was about the last thing she'd expected to hear.

"You can't be serious."

Noel blinked at Cooper, but she leaned into him slightly, and in that moment, Cooper knew he'd said the right thing.

"That's Cooper Meyer, Mom. For your list," Noel said, her tone even.

"I told your father for years that we should have put you in boarding school. It will always be one of my biggest regrets."

With that, Mrs. Echolls strolled out of the store and didn't look back. The chimes above the door sounded in the complete silence that followed.

Noel sagged a little. Her respiration rate increased, and her hands began to shake.

Without a word, Cooper led her to a chair and stood in front of her, taking both of her hands in his. "You're not alone." He could feel the tension in the panic attack that didn't seem to want to let her go.

She gasped for air as her face paled. She leaned forward,

and he let her rest her head against his chest. "Father God, I pray that You would reach down and touch Noel. Fill her heart and mind with peace." He continued to slowly rub circles across her upper back as he silently prayed for her.

Slowly, her breathing returned to normal, and she quit shaking. She finally leaned back and swiped at the tears that had escaped her eyes and were flowing down her cheeks.

"Is Noel sad?" Jett spoke from nearby, a concerned look on his face. He stepped forward and gave her a hug.

Cooper hadn't even realized that Jett had been watching them.

"Thank you, Jett. I'm feeling a little better now." She smiled at him, although Cooper could tell it was forced.

Jett held his reindeer close and sat in a chair nearby.

"I know what might help," Cooper announced. He reached into a box under the counter and pulled out the axolotl he'd given her a week ago when she'd come in with a panic attack. "Here."

Noel accepted it with a small smile. "Thank you." She ran a hand over the animal's soft head. She finally looked up and met Cooper's eyes. "You shouldn't have said anything. It was just for my parents' stupid Christmas party. I could've handled anyone she'd paired me with for one night."

"And now you don't have to."

"It's not that simple. My family isn't like yours, Cooper." She winced and pressed a finger to her temple. Then she glanced at Jett. "Look, I was going to help tonight, but I'm getting a headache. If I don't get on top of it, it'll turn into a migraine." She looked embarrassed at the mention of it. "Do you mind if I just go home?"

"Of course not." He stood close as she got up off the chair and reached down for her bag. "Is there anything I can do to help? I feel like I may have made things worse for you earlier. Did I make you angry by speaking up?"

"I'm not angry." She reached over and waved at Jett. "I'll see you later, okay? Take good care of Rudy."

"Bye, Noel." Jett waved, a look of sadness on his face.

Cooper followed her to the door. "Noel. Talk to me."

She glanced at Jett. "Now's not the time."

"Then I'll take him home and call you."

While Noel looked hesitant, she didn't say no. Instead, she handed him the axolotl.

"I'll call you as soon as I can. Okay?"

She gave him a barely perceptible nod. "Yeah."

Cooper's stomach clenched as he watched her climb into her car and drive away.

9

The moment Noel was in her car and driving away from the bookstore, the tears began to fall again. Never in a million years would she have expected her mother to track her down at the bookstore and show up like that.

The humility of having her there and talking down about the store collided with the confusion and frustration when Cooper told Mother that he was Noel's plus one.

He had no idea what he was getting into. Not only would her parents not approve of him, but they would be rude and obvious about it. He didn't deserve that.

The headache pounded behind her eyes as she parked in front of her house and went inside.

After taking some headache powder followed by a glass of water, she laid down on the couch, not even bothering to kick off her shoes.

Her eyes slid shut, and she allowed sleep to drown out the horribleness of the evening.

Noel wasn't sure how long she'd been asleep when her phone rang. Confused, she sat up and reached for it. There was a small list of people that she would answer the phone for, and she quickly realized once she saw Cooper's name that he was one of them.

She swiped to answer. "Hello?"

"Noel. Hey. Can we talk? Like sit down and have a conversation talk?"

A quick glance at the window told her it was dark outside. She glanced at her watch. "It's after eight." It was as much of a statement to herself as a response to Cooper.

"The pancake place on Tenth is open all night. I can swing by, pick you up, and we'll go get something to eat. I don't want to leave things where they are until tomorrow." There was no missing the sincerity in his voice.

Noel quickly took stock of how she felt. Her headache had eased, but her stomach was growling. And no, she didn't want to leave things the way they were, either.

"Okay."

"Awesome. What's your address?"

She gave it to him, and then, once they'd ended the call, she went to wash her face, brush her hair, and change into a clean shirt.

Less than ten minutes later, the doorbell rang.

Noel shrugged into a denim jacket and swung the door open to find Cooper waiting outside. He gave her a genuine smile, but he looked her over as though he wasn't sure what he was going to find.

"I didn't realize how close you were to the store and downtown." Cooper leaned back and looked at the house. "It's a nice place."

"Thank you. Yeah, most of the time, I walk everywhere and don't even bother driving my car." She grabbed her messenger bag and stepped through the doorway, closing and locking the door behind her.

Cooper put a hand against her back and guided her to his car. Once they were settled inside, he turned to look at her.

"I should have asked if you were okay with pancakes. We can look for somewhere else to eat."

"Are there people who don't like pancakes?" The question was mostly meant as a joke. But seriously, Noel wasn't sure she'd ever met someone who didn't like them.

He chuckled. "Not that I know of."

"Was Jett okay after I left?"

Cooper pulled his car away from the curb. "He was a little worried about you. But in general, he was pretty oblivious to the whole thing."

"That's good." She relaxed against the seat as they drove the rest of the way in silence.

As expected, the restaurant wasn't very busy. Their hostess seated them across from each other at a corner table in the back.

Noel opened the menu and perused the breakfast items. It didn't take long for them to decide and place their orders.

Cooper folded his hands on the table. "How's your head? Are you feeling okay?"

"The ache is dull. I took medication when I got home, and I seem to have avoided a migraine." This time. Noel wasn't always certain of the triggers. Although the cause was pretty clear this time. "I'm sorry I ran out like that. I was surprised. Embarrassed. I didn't handle it very well."

Noel should have insisted that they step outside to talk. Or maybe she should have called to let Mom know she wasn't bringing a plus one days ago. If she had, none of this would have happened.

And then Cooper wouldn't be on her mother's radar.

"Let me make one thing clear." Cooper paused when a glass of orange juice was set down in front of each of them.

He nodded his thanks to the waiter. "As far as I'm concerned, there's nothing for you to apologize for. I'm just sorry that I spoke up without knowing all the details. I hope I didn't make things worse for you or between you and your mom."

Noel gave an unladylike snort. "Well, things couldn't be that much worse between me and my parents, so no worries there." She took a sip of her orange juice. "They've chosen not to be a part of my life or Jace's in many different ways. But they expect us to come to this shindig of theirs. Friends and business partners they've known for years attend, and it's all for show. It's the one thing that Jace and I do for them. Just so we don't sever connection completely, you know?"

He watched her and waited patiently for her to continue.

"My mother is big on social propriety. You know, you're supposed to go to the party with your plus one. Well, Jace and I always attended together. But once he and Bonnie got married, my mother started pressuring me to bring someone. And I'm afraid I don't have an enemy I dislike enough to drag along with me."

Cooper had been taking a drink then and nearly choked. He covered his mouth with a napkin and coughed as he laughed. "I'm sorry. I know it's not funny."

Noel grinned. "Trust me, it has to be." She laughed along with him. When he'd finally stopped sputtering, she elaborated. "This year, apparently, my mother felt she'd waited long enough and gave me an ultimatum. Either I give her the name of someone I'm bringing with me, or she'll set me up with a guy when I arrive."

His jaw dropped. "This is like something from a movie. Are you serious?"

"As a heart attack." The waiter brought their meals and set them on the table. Noel looked at her stack of pancakes and the bacon beside it with appreciation. She started to spread butter on the pancakes as they talked. "Since I hadn't given her a name, I assumed that she'd just set me up with someone, and that would be that. If I can survive the party itself, I can survive having to sit beside someone I don't know." She poured maple syrup over the melting butter, and her stomach let out a low growl.

"It's definitely not your typical family Christmas party." Cooper drizzled ketchup on his hashbrowns and took a bite.

"You know the usual foods you have at Christmas? The warm fireplace, carols, and cookies for dessert?" She waited for him to nod. "Yeah, there's none of that. It's held in a huge, impersonal room with a twenty-foot-tall Christmas tree because it's expected. They serve sushi and shrimp and steak. Dessert is something I can't usually pronounce. If it weren't for the Christmas tree, it'd be just like any other business party they put on. The kind that Jace and I were never allowed to attend."

"It sounds dreadful."

Noel eyed him from across the table. She appreciated his honesty. "It truly is." She hesitated. "I have anxiety medication that my doctor gave me, but I haven't started it. I don't want to need it. But when I think about this party, I wonder if I should."

His food completely forgotten, Cooper reached across the table and rested his hand on her arm. "There is nothing wrong with needing medication for anxiety or anything else, Noel. Nothing. It's no different than seeking medical assistance to lower blood pressure or taking insulin for diabetes. If you need it, you need it."

His complete acceptance and lack of judgment unexpectedly brought tears to Noel's eyes. Eyes that were already aching from her crying stint earlier in the evening. She blinked rapidly and willed the moisture away.

"Thank you for that." Jace had always said the same thing. But her parents felt it was a weakness, and it was one that she should have control over.

"Maybe my being there will help a little this year."

"Like I said before. I don't have an enemy I dislike enough to take along, much less you." She moved her arm from beneath his and cut a bite of pancake with more force than was necessary. "I'll call my mother in the morning and let her know."

"Why not?"

When she didn't answer him, he set his fork down and leaned forward.

"Noel. I want to go with you. I promise I'll be on my best behavior. We'll make fun of the food. And when it's over, I'll take you out for burgers and fries. What do you say?"

BETWEEN MEETING NOEL'S mother and then seeing Noel's panic attack afterward, the idea of her going into that lion's den of a party was something Cooper wasn't comfortable with. He silently prayed that she'd agree to let him go with her.

He decided to switch tactics and see if he could entice a smile. "After that winning description of the party, I've got to see it for myself. You wouldn't deprive me of that memorable experience, would you?" He gave her his best puppy dog eyes.

It was clear she was trying to stay strong, but seconds later, she busted out laughing until her eyes were watering. "You are an absolute mess," she said when she could finally catch her breath.

Cooper took enormous satisfaction in the fact that he got her to laugh like that.

He grinned at her. "It was worth it." He raised an eyebrow. "Just for clarification, does that mean I can go to the party?"

"I guarantee you that you'll regret it. But yes. If you insist."

"I do insist. And if I'm going to be there with you, I can't possibly see how I would regret it."

From the way she blushed, it was clear she caught his flirting. Truthfully, he surprised himself. There was a lot about her that he didn't know, and obviously, that went both ways. But if there was one thing Cooper was certain about, it was that he wanted the chance to rectify that.

As they ate their meals, they talked about the bookstore, the most embarrassing Christmas gift they'd ever received, and then started comparing movies they'd seen recently.

Before they knew it, it was after eleven. Noel covered her third yawn in ten minutes.

Cooper waved down a waiter and paid for the bill. "Come on, let's get you home."

They were both quiet as he drove her back to her house and then walked her to the door.

After everything that happened at the bookstore, he hadn't wanted to leave things as they were. He was glad he'd suggested they get a late meal together.

"Until tomorrow evening?"

"Until then. Thanks again, Cooper."

"For what?" As far as he was concerned, she didn't need to thank him for anything. He'd like to think anyone would've been outraged when they saw the way Mrs. Echolls treated her daughter.

Noel shrugged as she looked down at her shoes. When

she finally raised her chin, she said just above a whisper, "When I have a panic attack, you don't make me feel weak."

"You are anything but weak, Noel." He reached out and brushed the back of his fingers against her cheek. It took everything inside him not to lean down and kiss her. But this connection with her was important, and he worried rushing things would be a mistake. Especially after how emotionally charged the day was. "Get some rest, okay?"

She nodded. "I will. You, too."

He brushed her cheek with his thumb and stepped back. He waited for her to get inside and lock the door before going back to his car.

10

I   t was early afternoon on Tuesday when Noel's name
    popped up on Cooper's cell phone. He answered the
    call immediately. "Hey. How's your day going?"

"It could be better." There was some shuffling in the
background. "I'm afraid I'm not going to be able to work at
the store today."

Her words dealt a heavy blow of disappointment. "Hey,
it's okay. You've been a huge help already, and I've just about
got everything ready. Thanks to you, opening on Thursday
night won't be a problem." It was completely true. But he
would have preferred to finish the store with her help. Especially because then she could see the final product before it
officially opened. "What's going on?"

"You know the big tree by the courthouse?"

"Sure." There was a community tree lighting every year
on the second weekend of November. He hadn't noticed the
tree this morning because he came into the center of town
from the opposite direction, but it stood one hundred feet tall
and was covered in lights and shiny ornaments.

"Someone vandalized it last night. The police may have

gotten a video of the people involved and are following up on it." There was a moment when she spoke to someone in the background. "Sorry about that. Anyway, we've had maintenance out all morning trying to fix it, but it's beyond repair. We're going to have to take the tree down and replace all the lights and many of the ornaments. A bunch of us are going to be working on that at the end of the day and into the evening."

Cooper couldn't imagine why someone would think to destroy such an iconic symbol of Christmas in Clearwater. Hopefully, the police would catch the people responsible. "Do you guys need some extra people to help?"

"Hold on just a second." She spoke to someone in the background again, but he couldn't quite hear what was being said. "Cooper? If you're really offering, we could definitely use some help." For the first time during their conversation, her voice sounded lighter.

He got the details about where to go and what time before hanging up.

Since Jett was currently at his day program and then would go home to their parents, the timing couldn't have been more perfect.

He focused on the store and got as much done as he could through the afternoon. At five o'clock, he drove to the other side of the square and parked on the side closest to City Hall.

A small crowd gathered around the Christmas tree which was laying on its side on the ground. For some reason, it looked even taller this way than it did when it was upright.

Cooper spotted Noel off to the side, planner in hand. The fact that she had it with her made him smile.

She noticed him as he approached, and her face brightened. "Hey. You made it."

"Of course." He took in her festive red and green sweater

and jeans. The chill in the air had made her cheeks red, and the green knit hat she wore framed her face perfectly. She looked beautiful. "So what can I do?"

It turned out that the vandals had destroyed the Christmas lights wrapped around the tree. Thankfully, the tree itself wasn't damaged. People had already taken all the Christmas decorations off, taken the artificial tree apart again, and then painstakingly unwrapped the old lights from each section.

By the time Cooper was there to help, they needed people to load the old lights into the back of a truck to be disposed of and then to wrap new lights tightly around the tree, section by section. The idea being that next year, each section would just need to be connected to each other and the entire thing would light up like before.

It was just like the artificial Christmas tree his family had put up year after year but on a much grander scale.

Each strand of lights was checked and double-checked. Once the lights had been replaced, the tree was put together again with the help of the Clearwater Fire Department.

Cooper stood beside Noel, and they watched as fire-fighters traversed the ladder to place each tree section on top of the other.

Noel slipped her hands into the pockets of her jeans as the air began to chill.

"You don't have a coat?" he asked her, thankful he'd brought his own.

She shook her head. "I didn't have this on my agenda when I left the house this morning."

And she'd probably walked to work, too.

Cooper pulled his coat off and held it out to her. When she started to protest, he gave her a firm look. "You're freezing, Noel."

She looked like she was going to argue until a shiver traveled through her. She chuckled and accepted his offer.

The coat was way too big for her, and she practically drowned in it. She also looked entirely too adorable. "It looks better on you than it does on me anyway," he joked.

She laughed at that. "Thank you."

When the tree was back in place, the firefighters began to add the decorations on the taller sections while members of the community used ladders to put the colorful orbs on the lower ones.

Noel and Cooper helped and then stood with the rest of the crowd when the tree was plugged in and the holiday beacon of Clearwater lit up the night once again.

A round of applause and cheering filled the air.

Cooper looked around them, proud of the way his community had stepped up to fix what someone else had tried to destroy.

It was well after eight when everyone started to disperse.

Cooper nudged Noel's arm with his own. "Since you didn't have your coat, would I be correct in assuming that you don't have your car nearby, either?"

A low chuckle was his answer. "I think it's getting dark early enough that I'll start driving my car to work until spring."

"I'm glad to hear that." He turned to look at her and admired the way the Christmas lights lit up her face. "Why don't I give you a ride home?"

She nodded once, and they turned toward the parking lot. Her hand brushed against his, sending sparks of awareness traveling up his arm. The second time, he reached out and captured it with his own and was happy when she didn't pull it away.

"I'll bet you're cold now," she said, her voice soft. "Thanks for letting me borrow your coat."

"It's pretty chilly. But it was worth it." He glanced at her and smiled.

"Your sacrifice is noted." She gave his hand a gentle squeeze.

They got to his car way too soon. If Cooper hadn't been so cold, he'd have been happy to walk her back to her house. As soon as they got inside, he cranked on the heater and then breathed a sigh of relief when it began to warm up less than a block from Noel's house.

She started to shrug out of the coat as soon as he parked, but he put a hand on her arm to stop her.

"Wear it up to the door. I'll get it from you there. No sense in you getting cold now."

He followed her and waited for her to unlock and open the door. Only then did he accept the coat. He hung it over his left arm.

Her gaze tangled with his. "I owe you. For the use of your coat. For helping me tonight. Helping us."

He gave her one of his playful smiles. "I know how you can pay me back." He paused long enough for her to give him a curious look before continuing. "By going with me to my parents' house for Thanksgiving lunch."

One of her eyebrows rose a smidge. "Go with you, huh?"

"I'll even come pick you up." He held his breath, praying she'd say yes. The location didn't matter, but getting to spend that extra time with her did.

"Okay."

"That's a yes, then?"

She rolled her eyes and tried to keep a straight face but failed miserably. "Yes. It's a yes."

Noel was starting to shiver, and if Cooper stayed any

longer, he was going to pull her into his arms and kiss her. Instead, he took a step back and raised a hand in a wave. "I'll call you tomorrow. Have a good night."

"You, too."

NOEL WATCHED out the window as Cooper drove them to his parents' house for Thanksgiving.

To say she was nervous was an understatement. She had changed outfits multiple times until she finally settled on a pair of jeans along with a long-sleeved tunic. The fabric was a light blue, which was one of Noel's favorite colors.

She kept telling herself that this was just lunch. She'd already met Cooper's family, and she wouldn't be the only guest.

As though he could hear her thoughts, Cooper reached over and took her hand in his. "I talked to my mom this morning. Our neighbor and my dad's friend will be there. Maple lives just down the street. Normally, she flies out to stay with her daughter for Thanksgiving. But her daughter's family is sick, so she'll fly down for Christmas instead. I'm glad she won't be eating alone today."

He laced his fingers with hers, and Noel marveled at the perfect way they fit together. The connection sent warmth straight to her heart. "What about your dad's friend?"

"Paul lost his wife ten years ago. They never had any kids. He has a Thanksgiving meal with our family almost every year." Cooper let go of her hand so that he could take a turn off Main Street. He glanced at Noel. "There were years I had no idea how many people would be at the table."

"That's really nice. Your parents..." Noel shook her head. She'd only met the Meyers once, and yet she already respected them far more than she ever had her own parents. "Your parents seem like very kind people."

Everyone invited to her parents' parties was chosen strategically. There's no way they'd invite someone just because they needed somewhere to go.

They reached the Meyer home, and Cooper escorted her to the door. When it swung open, Jett was there to grab one of each of their hands and pull them inside.

"It's Thanksgiving!" A smile lit up his face. "There's pumpkin pie." Then he lowered his voice as though sharing a secret. "But I hate turkey."

Noel smothered a giggle.

Then Mr. Meyer was there with a hearty handshake. Mrs. Meyer engulfed Noel in a hug that had her both stunned and suddenly wishing she'd grown up with someone that so freely gave hugs.

She was introduced to Paul and Maple. Then Mrs. Meyer whisked Noel away from the comfort of Cooper's side. "Will you help me with a couple of last-minute things, Noel?"

"Of course."

She wasn't much of a cook. Hopefully, Mrs. Meyer didn't need any help in that department. She swallowed the lump in her throat and wiped her sweaty palms on her jeans.

"I was wondering if you could keep stirring the gravy so it doesn't scorch while I finish up a couple of sides."

Noel accepted the whisk with relief. She could stir gravy. "Your home is lovely. Thank you so much for the invitation to join you."

Mrs. Meyer smiled warmly as she began to mash a pot full of steaming potatoes. "I'm glad you decided to join us. I hope you'll make yourself at home. I think you'll find we're very informal around here." She poured some milk into the pot and added a generous spoonful of butter.

They chatted about the weather and the bookstore while Mrs. Meyer finished getting the sides ready. It wasn't long before they were all seated around a large, rectangular table and praying over the bounty laid out before them.

"And thank You, Father, for the opportunity to share this meal with friends, both new and old. Amen." Mr. Meyer looked up from his prayer and gave a satisfactory nod around the table.

"Amen!" Jett said with gusto. He'd snagged the chair next to Noel's while Cooper sat on her other side. Jett turned to her and said, his tone serious, "You can have my turkey."

By the time three hours had passed, Noel was stuffed to the gills with a traditional Thanksgiving meal plus a huge slice of apple pie with generous amounts of cinnamon baked into it. She also couldn't remember the last time she laughed so much.

They were all seated in the living room visiting, except for Jett, who had gone to his room some time ago. Noel had chosen a spot on the sofa with Cooper to her right.

As the conversation flitted from one topic to the next, Noel not only felt included but incredibly welcomed. She wondered what it would have been like to grow up in a family like this one. It was almost impossible to imagine.

Her eyes misted, and she blinked them clear only to find Cooper watching her, his brows drawn together in concern. He put a hand on her shoulder and leaned close.

"Is everything okay?"

She nodded, unwilling to trust her own voice.

He watched her for another second or two, seemed convinced, then leaned away again. Before dropping his hand, he softly fingered a section of her hair.

It was such a little thing—and brief—but it made her want to lean into him and feel his warmth. Every time their arms brushed against each other, she remembered the way it felt when they held hands, and it took a great deal of control to not reach for his now.

"So, Noel," Maple spoke from her spot on the comfortable-looking recliner. "Your name is so beautiful. Were you born around Christmas? Or did your parents just love the name?"

"It was my grandmother's middle name," she said, the response practically rehearsed through the years.

Thankfully, everyone accepted the explanation without question, and the topic of conversation shifted quickly, freeing Noel from having to go into more details.

When it was time for them to leave, even Maple gave her a hug.

Noel settled into the passenger seat for the ride back to her place with two bags of leftovers nestled on the floorboard near her feet.

She watched as Cooper got behind the wheel and leaned back to pat his stomach. "I won't need to eat for a week," he told her with a groan.

"Me either," she agreed. "Everything was amazing."

Including him.

She clasped her hands in her lap and tried her best not to fiddle with the ring around one of her pointer fingers.

"Are you glad you came with me?" It was a normal question, but the way he was watching her, waiting for a response, made it seem as though it were a much more serious one.

"Yes, I am. Thank you for suggesting it. Over. And over." She gave him a wink, so he knew she was joking. "Your parents are some of the sweetest people I've ever met. Truly."

"I think they really liked you, too." He glanced at her as though what he'd just said was monumental. "Can I ask you a question?"

"Sure."

"Is Noel really your grandmother's middle name?"

So he had gotten the sense that there was more to the story. She bit the inside of her cheek. "It is. When Jace and I were born, they named us both after our paternal grandparents—the same ones we spent summers with." She paused. It'd been such a nice day that she hated to share anything that was negative. "I once heard them arguing about them when we were eleven or twelve. It turns out that our parents named us after them, hoping that, if they didn't end up in the will, at least we would."

Cooper looked about as shocked as she'd felt when she discovered the truth. "I have no words."

"It's okay, though, because they were more like parents than our parents ever were. I wouldn't have wanted to be named after anyone else anyway. But yeah, it hurt to hear that at the time." Noel gathered her hair together and pulled it over one shoulder. "If it all weren't so horrible, it would be funny that Jace and I were named in his will, and it still did my parents no good."

"It says a lot about you and your brother that you grew up to be nothing like your parents. And it says a lot about the kind of people that your grandparents were, too."

The kindness in his voice made Noel's heart stutter. "I appreciate that."

They pulled in front of her house. Cooper got out and went around so that he could open the door for her. "Will I see you at the Stroll?"

They walked up the pathway to her front door. "If last year was any indication, I'll be running around like a crazy person. But I'll drop by the store, even if it's just for a few minutes."

"I'll be watching for you. Try not to work too hard

tonight." He leaned forward and pressed a kiss to her cheek. With that, he turned and went back to his car.

Noel released the breath she didn't realize she'd been holding.

There was no denying it. She was falling for Cooper Meyer, and she had been since the first day she met him.

ince Cooper had never been one to go out shopping on Thanksgiving evening, he really had no idea what to expect from the Moonlight Stroll.

Colorful lights lit up the windows out front, and he had Christmas music playing in the background inside the store.

He'd even brought in a bowl to put on the counter and filled it with Hershey's kisses wrapped in red, green, and silver.

It was a good thing Jett stayed with their parents. Cooper had gone back and forth between imagining a few customers stopping by and worrying that no one would show up at all. He hadn't anticipated the number of people that came in and out over the course of the late evening.

Cooper lost track of how many people he met and how many times customers told him they were so glad he'd opened the bookstore.

The Moonlight Stroll lasted until midnight, and by the time eleven o'clock rolled around, Cooper had had to refill the candy bowl twice.

As successful as the grand opening seemed to be, he

hadn't yet seen the one person he was most looking forward to seeing come in.

Every time the chimes announced a new potential customer, he looked up, hoping to see Noel's beautiful face. There were many times he'd been busy wrapping up purchases, and he just hoped he hadn't missed her.

A half-hour later, the crowds were beginning to thin noticeably, and Cooper was starting to tidy things up a bit and get ready to close.

The front door opened, and Noel breezed through. She held a to-go cup in one hand while cupping the other over the top.

Cooper's heart soared in his chest, and he rounded the counter, his current task completely forgotten.

"There you are. I was hoping the evening was going as well out there as it has been in here."

Noel gave him a brilliant smile. "Everything seems to have come together without a hitch." She held the cup out and lifted the other hand to reveal two chocolate chip cookies balanced on the lid. "I didn't want you to miss out since I knew you hadn't been able to leave the store."

Her thoughtfulness seriously made his day. He took them gratefully. "You are a lifesaver." He polished off a cookie in two bites and motioned to a chair behind the counter. "I'll bet you're exhausted. Do you want to sit for a few minutes?"

Noel glanced at her watch. "I have about ten." She eased herself onto the chair and groaned. "Oh, my feet hurt." She turned her watch to show him how many steps it had recorded.

"I say that warrants taking the weekend off once you get through tomorrow." He offered her the other cookie, but she politely declined. "I'm really glad I didn't bring Jett here tonight. He would've been completely overwhelmed."

Truthfully, there had been several times that evening when Cooper wondered how he would handle keeping an eye on Jett and managing the store in the future when Jett was staying with him full-time. Cooper wouldn't always be able to handpick which days Jett came in and which he didn't unless he hired a manager at some point.

"What's wrong?" Noel was watching his face. And then, as though she could somehow sense his thoughts, she said, "You have time to ease into everything with Jett. Get used to running the bookstore first, then you'll know better how to bring Jett into it."

He reached for her hand. "You are a very wise woman." He brought her hand to his mouth and brushed a kiss across her knuckles before releasing it again. "So, tell me about your evening so far."

"To start with, our tree is still standing and beautiful. Those chocolate chip cookies I gave you were the last two, so I've made a note to have more cookies available next year. Oh!" She put her feet on the floor with a slap. "You won't believe what I saw." She pulled her phone out of her pocket, flipped through photos, and then showed one to him. "Mr. Brooks did this all on his own."

Cooper took her phone and looked at the photo. In the window hung a lone model airplane outlined with Christmas lights. "So he decided to decorate after all." He handed the phone back to her.

"It's no toy soldiers flanking the door, but I'll take it." She looked satisfied as she stuffed the phone back into her pocket and stood. "I'd better get back out there."

"And you brought your car so you can drive home?"

She flashed him a look of mock annoyance. "Yes, I have my car here."

"Good. Otherwise, I'd offer to drive you home myself. I could wait for you regardless."

A little smile played at the corners of her mouth. "I appreciate that, but I may be later. There's no need for you to hang around. I'm sure you're tired, too."

He was, but he didn't like the idea of her being out after midnight all by herself. "Will you at least text me when you get home?" He stood so he could walk her to the door.

"I can do that." She took a last look around the bookstore. "It really does look great, Cooper."

"And you look beautiful, Noel. I should have told you that when I picked you up for lunch." He took a step closer to her. "And this bookstore wouldn't be where it is now without you."

He put an arm lightly around her lower back and leaned in. His lips were a breath away from hers when the chime sounded, announcing another customer.

It was all he could do to contain a groan of disappointment. Instead, he pulled her close for a brief hug. "Text me when you get home. And I'll talk to you tomorrow?"

She nodded into his shoulder before stepping back. "Good night, Cooper."

"Good night." He watched her exit his store before turning to the older couple who had wandered in. "Welcome to Book Haven! Is there anything I can help you with?"

"I'M NEVER FLYING with young children again," Bonnie groaned as she took a load of laundry out of the dryer.

"That's what you said last time." Noel tried not to chuckle.

"Well, we only had Gunner then." Bonnie transferred

clothes from the washing machine into the dryer, closed the door, and turned it on. "This time, I mean it."

It was Monday evening, and Jace's family had only been home since late Saturday. Since they'd been back, there'd been an issue with the sheep requiring Jace to be out all day and possibly well into the night.

Noel was hoping to see Cooper, but the bookstore was open until eight tonight, and he'd been busy all afternoon and evening with customers. Which was a good thing, but it meant that, just like the weekend, they'd been like ships in the night when it came to their schedules and not being able to do more than wish each other a passing "hello."

So Noel thought she might help Bonnie with the kids, bring dinner by so she didn't have to cook and see how their trip was.

"But everything was fine once you actually got there?"

Bonnie put the basket of clothes on the coffee table. "It really was," she said with a smile. "I am glad we went. Who knows when I'll get the chance to see my great-aunt again."

Noel reached for clothing to fold, but Bonnie put out a hand to stop her. "Trust me, that'll still be there later. Come on, let's get a cup of tea and sit for a few minutes."

"You won't get an argument from me." The last few days had been a blur. Thursday's Moonlight Stroll was a success. Friday was super busy as everyone switched gears in antici-pation of A Country Christmas, which was less than two weeks away. Noel had a list a mile long that made her stressed out when she thought about it. Then, Saturday, she'd helped Wyatt and Chrissy with some things at the stables.

All in all, she was exhausted and would be ready for another weekend if the coming one didn't also mean her parents' Christmas party.

She held the cup of tea in her hands and carefully sipped

the herbal liquid. Tea wasn't her favorite drink, but she did appreciate the calming effect it usually had on her. She'd often thought about leaving coffee behind but never could quite do it.

The sounds of Gunner playing with a racetrack came from the other room. Grayson was sleeping soundly in a portable crib in the living room where the women had settled.

Bonnie took a quick look at her young son. "He's going to be up half the night. The trip messed up his whole sleep schedule."

"It'll straighten itself out." Although Noel knew that was easier said than done.

Bonnie took a sip of her tea and studied Noel over the edge of the cup. "So, how are things with Cooper?"

Noel wanted to deny that there even was a "thing," but she knew that the blush in her cheeks had already betrayed her.

"How did our parents not scare you away from Jace?"

Bonnie barely set her teacup down without spilling as she laughed. "Well. It helps that Jace is nothing like them. And that I'm used to standing up to my own parents who, while not quite as interesting as yours, didn't exactly win any parent of the year awards either." She paused. "This is about Cooper going with you to the party on Saturday."

"There's a potential something there between us. But every time I let myself even think about the possibility, I picture him running for the hills once my parents eviscerate him at the party."

With a shake of her head, Bonnie picked up her cup again. "If that scares him away, then he wasn't going to stick around anyway. Honestly? It's a great test. If he's willing to keep seeing you after Saturday, he'll be a keeper." There was humor in her voice.

"Funny."

"I am being silly. But there's a grain of truth there, too. Life is messy, Noel. No matter how you look at it. But we wouldn't appreciate the beauty of it if we didn't have something to compare that to." She shrugged. "Cooper is probably worrying about similar things. From what you said, his family sounds great. But if things work out between you and the two of you get married, you'd be signing up as one of Jett's caretakers for the rest of your life. That's not a small thing to ask of someone."

Noel hadn't thought about it that way. Could she step in as a primary caregiver for Jett? The very thought, with all of its unknowns, gave her pause. There were times, with her anxiety, that she wondered if she would even make a good mother at all, much less be a mother figure or big sister to an individual with special needs.

"Hey." Bonnie nudged Noel's foot with hers. "I wasn't trying to bring you down. Just trying to say that you probably aren't the only one who is unsure about everything. That doesn't mean it won't work or that God doesn't have it all planned out."

"Yeah. I know." She did, but it was good to get the reminder. "Well, we discovered that we work well together while getting the bookstore put together. I guess the party will be phase two." She looked at Bonnie. "You're always so calm and collected when you're around our parents."

Bonnie laughed outright. "That's because I've probably heard all of their insults by now, and I have a long list of semi-polite responses to counter them with. Trust me, I go through conversations in my head for days before this party. Besides, Jace is worth it." She winked.

Grayson started fussing, and Bonnie stood to go get him. "I'll be praying for you and Cooper."

"Thanks, Bonnie." Noel barely had time to set her cup on the coffee table before Gunner raced across the room and jumped onto her lap. "Will you read this to me, Auntie?" He held out a book about dinosaurs.

"Of course I will, buddy."

12

"I hired two people to help me out at the bookstore," Cooper said as he and Noel walked down Main Street toward the small park on the other side of the square. "I'm hoping one of them will work out well enough that I can train him or her to be an assistant manager after the new year." He glanced down at their joined hands. It was already Thursday, and he'd barely seen Noel all week.

He knew starting a new business would take a great deal of time and money. He thought he'd been prepared for it and had assured his parents that he could handle helping with Jett as well.

Until he met Noel.

She spent her Sundays with her brother and his family. And the only other day that Cooper had off—Mondays—was the day that Noel was often the busiest at work.

"I think that's great, Cooper. Hopefully, that will help take some of the pressure off of you. Especially when the store gets really busy."

They crossed the street and entered the park. It mostly consisted of manicured shrubs and several benches situated around flower beds that were full of blooms in the spring and summer. The only flowers thriving now were pansies.

"I'm ready for things to calm down a little." He lifted their hands and brought hers to rest against his chest.

He'd thought about their near kiss in the bookstore many, many times. Thanks to their schedules, finding time to spend together without other people around for one reason or another had been a challenge.

This is why, when the opportunity to go for a walk presented itself, he jumped at the chance and was pleased to see she did as well.

"I am, too. And I'm ready for Saturday to be over."

He knew she was dreading her parents' party. He'd already gone over all the details with her on what he should wear and when to pick her up. Making sure he had a party gift to take along that they wouldn't turn their nose up at (and refusing to allow Noel to pay for it).

He was as ready as he could be.

"You can still back out."

Cooper stopped and tugged on her hand until she was standing right in front of him. "I'm not backing out."

"I wouldn't blame you. I promise we can still be friends."

There was humor in her voice, but Cooper had no doubt that she was partially serious, too.

"Noel, I'm not backing out. And your parents aren't going to change the way I see you." He put his arms on her shoulders and leaned in closer. "Unless I'm reading things wrong, I think there's potential for whatever this is between us to be more than just friendship." He noted the way the pulse in her neck fluttered. "Am I wrong?"

"No. You're not wrong," she said, her voice just above a whisper.

"Good." There was no hesitation as he kissed her, softly at

first. When she leaned into him and cupped the back of his neck with one hand, he pulled her closer before deepening the kiss.

Everything about her, from the way her hair slid between his fingers to the way she smelled faintly of cinnamon, was perfect.

Reluctantly, he broke the kiss. They caught their breath as their gazes tangled.

The spark of appreciation in Noel's eyes shifted to one of humor. "I'll kiss you again if you change your mind about the party."

"Not on your life." He pressed a much shorter but more intense, kiss to her lips. "Come on, it's late, and it's getting cold out here." He put an arm around her shoulders and tugged her to his side.

ONE HOUR DOWN. Two to go.

There was no doubt in Noel's mind that her mother had expected her to show up at the Christmas party without Cooper. She barely gave him a nod of acknowledgment when they came in and hadn't paid him a smidge of attention since.

That was just fine as far as Noel was concerned. It was better to be ignored than insulted.

Mother's treatment of Bonnie was only slightly better, and only because most of their friends and business acquaintances knew that she was married to Jace by now. If Mother were too rude to Bonnie, it wouldn't look good. Even still, after a kiss on each cheek and one of the fakest hugs known to man, Bonnie was dismissed.

Now Noel, Cooper, Jace, and Bonnie sat at a table

together with tiny plates that they had to fill multiple times at the food table in order to even remotely get enough to eat.

Cooper leaned over and lowered his voice. "Okay, I'm going to ask. What is the gray paste?"

"It's a pâté," Noel and Jace answered in sync.

"I'd gathered that." Cooper chuckled. "But what kind?"

"One we've yet to identify." Jace pointed to the other three plates. "Please note that none of us have the gray paste on our plates. I recommend conveniently disposing of it for your own safety."

Bonnie, who had been trying to keep back her laughter, had to bury her face in her husband's shoulder to muffle her giggles.

Wyatt and Chrissy were keeping their boys for the evening so that the couple could have a rare night out. It was too bad they had to spend it here instead of doing something more enjoyable. Still, Noel always enjoyed seeing Jace and Bonnie together.

Music began to play, and Father announced that the dance floor was now open. Jace didn't hesitate to sweep his wife away.

Cooper leaned back in his chair and watched as they, along with several other couples, began to dance in the center of the room. "I like your brother, Noel. He seems to be a really nice guy. And Bonnie seems great, too."

Noel smiled in Jace's direction. "I'm thankful we've always had each other." She nodded toward her parents. "As far as the dancing goes, it usually signals that the party is half over. Which is worth celebrating all on its own."

"And what about you? Do you usually dance as well?"

"I usually find a dark corner to disappear into until the next act of tonight's production."

Cooper took her hand and kissed it. "But what about this year?"

"This year, I believe I'll make an exception."

A brilliant smile lit up her face as she stood and allowed Cooper to escort her to the dance floor.

He held her close while they slowly swayed to the music.

Cooper leaned just far enough back to take a look at the light green dress that hung down to Noel's ankles. "You look gorgeous tonight."

"Thank you, kind sir. And you look like a handsome prince."

At that, he gave her a nod of thanks.

Dancing with Cooper was a wonderful distraction that Noel didn't normally have at her parents' party, and she was rather sad when the last song faded.

She started to step away from Cooper, but he caught her around the waist and placed the lightest of kisses on her lips. With a smile, he led her back to the table they shared with Jace and Bonnie.

They all happily took a seat and enjoyed something to drink.

"Now, what's next?" Cooper asked in a quiet tone.

"Mingling," Jace and Bonnie said together.

"Also known as our cue to watch for a convenient escape route," Noel elaborated. "The key is to get in a conversation with our parents while they are talking to someone else as well. That's when we let them know that we're heading out."

Jace nodded his agreement. "And since other guests are there, they can't berate us for leaving too early."

Cooper looked to Bonnie. "They've got this down to a science."

"That they do."

Noel excused herself to go to the restroom before they

looked for their opportunity to escape the party. But as she was coming out, she jumped when she found her mother standing there waiting for her.

"I hope you're happy," she said in that tone that made it clear that she was not.

There were any number of things that her mother might have been disappointed about, but Noel had no doubt Cooper was at the heart of the problem tonight.

"I think the party turned out lovely this year. The tree is especially beautiful."

"You had your fun bringing him here tonight. I'm going to tell you right now, so that you have plenty of time, that I expect you to be serious next year."

Whenever Noel thought she'd seen her mother at her lowest, Leslie Echolls surprised her. "And what if he's the one, Mom?"

Her mother looked positively appalled. "It's bad enough that your brother went and married the help. I expect much better of my daughter."

Noel frowned as a sadness settled over her heart. "Then I'm afraid you may be disappointed."

"I don't want to see Cooper Meyer at another family function." The words were spoken coldly. Firmly. Because she fully expected Noel to comply.

Noel strode forward and gave her mother a hug. "Then that will include me, too. Goodbye, Mom. I do love you. Please know and remember that."

She tried to ignore the band that constricted around her chest, making it difficult to breathe, as she walked purposefully from the restroom toward the table where the others were waiting.

The moment Jace caught her eye, he jumped to his feet. He was the first to reach her. "What happened?" He gently held on to one of her arms.

Cooper cupped her other elbow. "Noel? Are you okay?"

Noel shook her head. "I .... need .... outside...."

"I'll get our coats," Bonnie told them and hurried away.

"Come on," Jace began, "let's get you out of here."

Noel pointed in Bonnie's direction. "Mom ... don't leave Bonnie alone..."

"I've got her," Cooper promised Jace and then whisked Noel from the room and into the cold air outside. He led her to a concrete bench, where she took a seat and willed the panic to subside.

Even though it seemed everything else was somewhere on the periphery, she was aware of the way Cooper's hands clasped hers, giving her something to focus on. Gradually, the blood rushing in her ears slowed as did her breathing. When she finally opened her eyes, she found Cooper kneeling on the ground in front of her, his gaze on her face.

"There you go." He stood up and placed a kiss on the crown of her head before sitting down beside her.

Noel concentrated on the feeling as he rubbed small circles on her back.

Jace had an arm around Bonnie's shoulders as they approached. A frown marred his face that only shifted to concern when he saw Noel.

"Are you okay?"

Noel nodded, suddenly feeling exhausted. "Yeah."

"What happened?" Cooper asked as he looked from one sibling to the other.

A slow smile spread across Jace's face. "According to my mother, Noel refuses to listen to reason and is throwing a hissy fit like a child."

Noel took in a slow breath. "I was informed that I needed to make a different choice when it came to who I brought to the next family function." She didn't meet Cooper's eyes.

"What else did she say?" The question came from Jace.

Noel had no desire to spread her mother's horrible words any further, but Bonnie laid a hand on her shoulder. "It's okay. It's nothing I haven't heard before."

With tears in her eyes and a renewed anger boiling in her belly, Noel looked up. "She said it was bad enough that Jace married the help. That she expected better things from me."

Jace clenched his fist before he put an arm around Bonnie and held her close. "And I have to know what you said. Because there's no way she'd be this angry if you'd just walked away."

Noel finally risked a glance at Cooper. "I told her she'd have to be disappointed."

Jace clapped his hands together. "Good for you. Well, when she told me that I needed to talk some sense into you, I told her that whatever stand you took, I'd be right there with you."

He pulled Noel off the bench and into a tight hug. "I'm proud of you, Noel. We should've walked out years ago."

"You wanted to," she reminded him. She was the one who had insisted that they needed to put in the effort once a year and not cut their parents out of their lives entirely. Except she was finally realizing their parents were the ones who were making that choice.

"You know what this means, don't you?" Bonnie asked, humor lacing her voice. "No more having to avoid the gray pâté next year." She poked Jace in the chest with a single finger. "Although it wouldn't kill us to go dancing once in a while."

Jace gave his wife a kiss that was just long enough to

make Noel look away. When she did, she caught Cooper watching her, his eyes shining. "You are something else."

They all looked at each other and laughed.

"What now?" Jace asked.

"Well," began Cooper, "I promised this lady here a burger and fries after the party. Anyone else game?"

13

N oel didn't even have to open her eyes to know that her migraine had persisted through the night and into Sunday morning.

The evening before, she, Cooper, Jace, and Bonnie had gone out for burgers and fries after the Christmas party fiasco. By the time they had reached the restaurant, she could feel the warning signs. Still, she hoped eating might help.

Unfortunately, by the time they had finished the meal, the migraine was hitting hard.

Noel had heard Jace telling Cooper about the migraines and what sometimes helped and didn't, but her head was pounding too much to really pay attention.

Cooper took her home, made sure she got inside okay and then tried to do what he could to help. She had finally told him she just needed sleep.

He'd kissed her on the forehead and left, albeit reluctantly.

Sometimes sleep helps to get rid of a migraine. But other times, it hung on for the next day. Sometimes even the day after that.

When Noel tried to sit up and felt like she'd be sick, she knew this was a particularly bad one. She called Jace to let him know she wouldn't make it to church. There was no way she could even drive there, much less sit through the service.

She'd rest and do whatever she could to, hopefully, make it go away before tomorrow. With A Country Christmas coming up in less than a week, she couldn't afford to miss a day of work.

She kept all the lights off in her house and the blinds closed. As much as she would prefer to stay in bed, she took a hot shower with essential oils that sometimes helped. Then, she ate a caffeinated breakfast bar and had a glass of juice before lying back down again.

A knocking at the front door woke her up. At first, Noel wasn't sure what time it was. A glance at the clock told her it was just after noon.

When she stood up, her head didn't pound nearly as bad as it had earlier.

She tried to run her fingers through her hair, vaguely remembering that she fell back to sleep while it was still damp. At least she'd gotten dressed so that she was somewhat presentable.

Or at least so she thought until she looked through the peephole and saw Cooper standing there. She groaned as she unlocked and opened the door.

The light from outside made her flinch. She backed up and held the door open. "Come on in at your own risk."

Cooper quickly closed it behind him. "I take it you still have a migraine." His voice sounded concerned.

"It's a little better now than it was this morning and last night." She patted her head and wished she'd grabbed a hat. "I know my hair is a mess."

"Are you kidding? You look beautiful." He put an arm

around her shoulders and a gentle kiss on her temple. "I know you're not up to company, but I wanted to bring a couple of things by. Including a hot chocolate with cinnamon, which your friend at the bakery said you like."

Noel accepted the drink and wrapped her hands around the warm cup. She took a whiff of the steam coming through the spout and sighed happily. "This is amazing."

"Oh, that's just the beginning." He gave her a grin. That's when Noel noticed he was carrying a large canvas bag.

He went to the kitchen table and started unpacking it. "I brought you two cinnamon scones. Plus, your friend insisted on sending an eggnog scone for you to try." He set them on the table. "A bowl of chicken noodle soup that's still hot but will be just fine rewarmed if you want it later, and some crackers." Cooper even unpacked a plastic spoon. "I don't know that much about migraines, but it said that sometimes caffeine helps. So I brought you two bottles of Coke and...." he reached into the bag and pulled out a large bag of peanut M&Ms, "...chocolate because I'm convinced that can help make anything better."

With that, he folded the canvas bag and slipped it under one arm.

Noel stared at the bounty on the table and slowly shook her head. "This is amazing, Cooper. I don't even know what to say."

"Just promise me that if your head doesn't feel better tonight, you'll text me and let me know so I can bring you dinner or something. Okay?"

"I'll send you an update late this afternoon," she promised. He did all of this for her? His kindness warmed her even more than the hot chocolate did. "Thank you."

"You're welcome." He stepped closer then and swept some hair away from her forehead. "I hate seeing you hurt

like this. Get some rest. I'll be praying you feel better soon."
He dipped his head to brush the lightest of kisses against her
lips.

With that, he gave her a wave and left. Noel stared at the
closed door in awe. Not only had he thought of nearly everything, but he hadn't tried to stay any longer than necessary.
There was no way she could've carried on a conversation for
long if he had.

She took another sip of her hot chocolate and closed her
eyes. "Thank you, Father, for bringing Cooper into my life."

"WHAT IS THIS?" Cooper asked when Noel handed him a
flyer on Tuesday. He didn't get to see her at all on Monday.
Thankfully, she felt better enough to go to work, though he
wished she had another day to rest up a little. But between
him being off work and helping his parents and her trying to
get caught up with everything, they never could coordinate
their schedules.

Today, she'd brought her lunch by the bookstore. They ate
together at the desk in the small office and listened for the
chimes announcing customers.

A large photo of a live reindeer adorned the flyer. Across
the top were the words, "Meet Santa and His Reindeer Event
for Families with Special Needs."

Noel smiled. "I talked to Wyatt about how Jett wanted to
see a live reindeer but that things were way too crowded and
busy at A Country Christmas. Trying to find a way to incorporate a special needs night on the square would be difficult
with such short notice. But Wyatt thought it would be a great
idea, so he offered to host it at the stables."

Cooper scanned the flyer. Not only would Santa and a live

reindeer be present, but it was indoors, quiet, and limited to individuals with special needs and their families.

The very idea that she'd pulled something like this together for his brother made Cooper's heart expand in his chest. "This is amazing, Noel."

"Now, I know the event is from five to seven, and your bookstore is open until eight on Fridays. But I can stay and manage it for the last few hours. I don't mind. That way, your whole family can go together."

"What about getting things finalized for A Country Christmas the next day?"

Noel shrugged. "There have to be priorities. I will let everyone know where I am, and I can coordinate some things by phone if need be."

There were no words. Instead, Cooper closed the distance between them with a kiss that had his pulse racing by the time he leaned back again. "Thank you."

"You're welcome." Noel shifted closer and kissed him again.

This right here. Everything about it felt right. Perfect.

"For the record," he said, his voice a whisper, "a guy could get real used to this."

He would have kissed her again if the chime hadn't sounded from the front of the store.

"Stay here and finish your lunch. I'll be right back." With that, he tapped the tip of her nose and jogged out to see if his new customer needed any assistance.

JETT CLUTCHED Rudy in his arms as they got out of the car at Joyful Hope Stables. Cooper kept an eye on Jett while Dad went around to help Mom. With everything that had happened over the last few months, they had done very little as a family unit. To be able to do this together was something Cooper didn't take lightly.

And it wouldn't have been possible if it weren't for Noel. Not just because she'd set the event up in the first place. But because if she weren't watching the store, he wouldn't be there right now.

He only wished she were walking by his side.

Jett was still nervous about going in the building, but not nearly as much as he was when they came to decorate cookies. Their parents were on either side of him, and Cooper took out his phone to snap a couple of pictures. Then he went to video. If Jett got as excited about the live reindeer as Cooper thought he might, then he wanted a video to show Noel later.

Wyatt greeted them at the entrance and shook Jett's hand. Cooper introduced his parents.

They kept their visit short, though, because Jett was craning his neck as he tried to see what was ahead. "Where's the reindeer?"

Wyatt chuckled. "Noel told me how much you like them. Come on, buddy, I'll show you. We've actually got two visiting us tonight."

Jett jumped up and down. "There are two?"

Cooper lagged behind just enough to record everything as they followed Wyatt.

There was no missing the stable area that had been set up ahead. Cooper was sure there was probably a better place outside, but then it would have been within sight of the horses. That it was indoors like this was surely thanks to Noel and her attention to detail.

Jett gave an exaggerated gasp and covered his mouth with one hand as the two reindeer came into view. "Dad! Reindeer. Real reindeer. Look!"

The wonder on his little brother's face brought tears to Cooper's eyes. He stopped the video and reached to shake Wyatt's hand. "Thanks for this, man. Truly."

"We do this for people just like Jett," Wyatt said. "They remind us to slow down and appreciate everything around us." He took one last look at Jett and made his way back to the entrance of the building.

Cooper took photos as Jett listened to the keeper tell him facts about the reindeer. He was hesitant at first, but Jett finally reached out and ran a hand down a reindeer's nose. He even got to feed the other a baby carrot.

It was an amazing experience and one Cooper knew his brother would treasure for years to come.

They offered to take Jett to see Santa or look at the other things at the event, but he wasn't interested. Instead, he happily held Rudy in his arms as they walked back to the car.

When everyone was ready, Cooper started the engine and headed back to his parents' house.

"And Noel set that up," Mom commented from the back seat.

Cooper raised his head enough to see her in the rearview mirror. There was no missing the tears in her eyes. "Yep."

"She's pretty special, Cooper."

"I know, Mom. I know." He was beginning to have a hard time picturing a future without her in it.

14

I t was a good thing the bookstore wasn't too busy Friday night because Noel was constantly on the phone with the teams that were putting the finishing touches in place for A Country Christmas tomorrow night.

There were several times when she refused to answer her phone at all so that she could concentrate on a customer. The last thing she wanted was to give a poor impression of the store and leave the customer not wanting to come back.

She'd just placed a purchased book and a plush in a plastic bag and wished a customer good evening when Arlene came into the store.

Arlene smiled, but the emotion didn't quite reach her eyes. "You're still here?"

"I am. Potentially until eight, depending on when Cooper gets back." Noel hadn't asked Arlene's permission first before coming to cover the bookstore. Since she didn't start until after five, it should've been okay. But Noel realized that she probably should have checked with her boss first. "I didn't start work here until I was technically off the clock."

Arlene took in the bookshop and then focused on Noel, a

frown on her face. "You know full well there's no such thing as 'off the clock' the evening before the biggest event of the year."

"And I've been working on that like crazy here, too." Noel lifted her work planner for emphasis.

There was a long pause. "I'm going to need you to be on board and focused tomorrow."

The insinuation was that she hadn't been lately. Or at least today. Given the long hours Noel had put in and the fact that everything was running according to plan, she felt like it was a completely unfounded opinion.

"We're on track, Arlene. Everything is under control. But this, tonight, was something I needed to do."

Arlene didn't look convinced. "After the holidays, we need to sit down. Outline the best way to combine your job with Elsie's. That way, we both know what to expect."

Noel hadn't officially decided on the job change. All she knew was that every time she thought about it, her stomach knotted up. She kept thinking that she might feel differently about it after the holidays. But next year would be just like this.

Suddenly, the decision seemed obvious.

"I can't take on Elsie's job, Arlene. I'm sorry. I'll be happy to stay on through January until you can find and train someone else to take my place."

Arlene's eyes widened. She looked like she wanted to argue, but she must have seen something in Noel's face that told her it wasn't up for discussion. "Okay."

Noel's phone rang. "It's Curt about the horse-drawn sleigh. I need to take this." She gave Arlene a genuine smile and answered the phone. By the time the conversation was over, Arlene was gone.

Usually, Noel created all kinds of lists when it came to

making important decisions. Putting in her notice like that without taking the time to officially weigh the pros and cons was not normal. It went against her instincts.

But the immense relief washing over her now told Noel that she had done the right thing.

She continued to balance the bookstore and work until Cooper came in at almost seven o'clock. He seemed surprised by the number of people milling about the store. He barely said hello before tossing a backpack into the office and jumping in to help Noel with customers.

It was a full twenty minutes before things settled down enough for them to talk.

"Has it been this busy the whole time?" he asked her.

"It's been relatively steady, but nothing like that. I guess you had perfect timing."

"I guess so." He threaded his fingers through the hair at the nape of her neck and leaned in for a slow kiss. "I missed you."

Noel placed the palm of one hand on his chest. "I missed you, too. And I'm really glad you came back when you did. How were the reindeer? Did Jett have fun?"

"I wish you had been there, Noel."

She listened, hands clasped against her chest, as he told her all about Jett's excitement. The video of Jett seeing the reindeer for the first time made every last effort to put the event together totally worthwhile. "Oh, he looks so happy."

"I think you might have made his year." Cooper slipped the phone into a back pocket. "Thank you for caring about Jett. For seeing him for who he really is."

"He's a great guy. Someone who has a lot to offer the world and deserves a chance to do just that." She meant every word of it, too.

He shook his head. "You are amazing. I hope you realize

that." He reached for her hand and rubbed the back of it with his thumb. "So, how was your evening?"

"Well, I put in my notice with my boss."

Cooper's eyebrows rose at the same time that Noel's phone rang.

She answered it to discover that one of the crews on the other side of the square had run into a snag with an electrical issue. "I'll be right there," she told them and hung up.

She'd much rather spend time here with Cooper, but after Arlene's visit earlier, she really should go and make sure everything was fixed and working properly.

"I'm sorry, I have to run." She shrugged into her coat and pulled up the zipper.

"And I'm sorry I didn't get a chance to hear the story behind you quitting your job. Call me when you get home?"

"It might be late."

"I don't care."

"Then I'll call you."

ONCE COOPER CLOSED up the bookstore, he decided to take a walk around the square instead of heading home. The idea of just sitting around and waiting for Noel to call didn't appeal to him at all. He'd much rather see if there was anything he could do to help instead.

He found Noel across the street from the town Christmas tree, talking to two other people. She gave them a wave and turned, spotting him in the process.

"Hey, what are you doing out here?"

"I thought I'd come and see if you needed any help."

"That's very sweet, but I think we've got everything under control. I'm sending everyone home for the night. There's no need to be out here any later when we have all day to put the rest of the fires out."

"So you're free to go home?"

"And more than ready." She pointed to the device behind her. "We couldn't get the snow machine to work, which was going to be a big issue. But it turned out to be a wiring problem, which was easily fixed."

Cooper had heard about the artificial snow and seen pictures of it. It was more like dense bubbles. It sure looked neat, though, and the kids seemed to love it. Clearwater didn't get a lot of real snow in the winter, so anything that resembled it was a treat.

"I'll bet you are tired." So was he, truth be told. "But the question is, are you too tired for pancakes?"

Noel laughed, and the beautiful sound floated around them. "Not even possible."

He held an arm out, and she took it as they walked across the square to his car. "Tell me what happened with your job."

Cooper drove them to the restaurant while she told him about the conversation she'd had with Arlene.

"The thing is, I want to do something I love, you know? Not something I'm stressed out about on a daily basis. And it would come to that if I had to manage my work along with what Elsie did. I can't blame Arlene for wanting to combine jobs, but it's not for me."

He'd thought a lot about Noel and her family after meeting them at the Christmas party. It was clear they had a lot of money, and he doubted Noel was the exception.

"Would I be right in assuming that you don't have to work if you don't want to? Financially speaking." He glanced at her profile and prayed he hadn't offended her.

She hesitated. "I have a decent savings account. But I refused to take anything from my parents once I turned eighteen. And anything my grandparents left us is tied up in the ranch." She looked at him. "No, I don't have to work. Not technically. But it would drive me crazy if I just sat around at home all day."

He admired that about her. "So you had to have had things you wanted to do when you were a kid. What did you want to be when you grew up?"

When she hadn't answered even after he'd parked the car and turned off the engine, he turned to face her. "Come on, what was the one thing you always dreamed of doing?"

"I told you that Jace and I were pretty much raised by nannies. That we almost never went on trips or vacations with our parents." She paused. "I guess I always dreamed of being a mom. You know, the kind that was waiting in the kitchen with chocolate chip cookies when the kids got home from school. The kind of mom her daughter could talk to. I wanted to marry someone who was involved with the kids, too. Then we would take our kids on big family vacations where we went to exotic places and made memories together." She shrugged. "But since I'm thirty-five and it's still just me, I try to stay busy and find ways to feed some of my hobbies."

"Like organizing events and helping the kids at the stables." So much made sense. Noel could have come through a childhood like that with all kinds of chips on her shoulders, many of them legitimate. Instead, she'd been able to walk away from a less-than-idyllic childhood with enthusiasm and a desire to make a difference.

"Exactly. Maybe having my own family isn't in the cards. But I can live vicariously through Jace and Bonnie and the kids. Then there's the stables. As long as I have plenty to keep me busy, I'm okay." She released her seat belt and moved to get out of the car.

Cooper caught up with her, and together they walked into

the restaurant. Once they were seated and had ordered, he continued the conversation where they'd left off.

"I get it. I'm only a year older than you, but I've wondered the same thing about having a family of my own. I mean, I don't regret my decision to care for Jett for the rest of my life. But that can be a pretty hard sell for someone else. Someone who is walking into a caregiver position that lasts a lifetime."

Noel had mentioned going on big vacations with the whole family. Jett had never done well in hotels or sleeping away from his own bed. Cooper couldn't imagine taking him on an extended family vacation and it being successful in any way.

He'd grown up admiring his parents for their love and commitment to each other and their family. But he'd also seen how they almost never went anywhere, just the two of them. And those big trips couples are supposed to take once they retire? They never had that, either.

Cooper knew they were happy with their life just like he was happy to care for his brother.

But Noel ... she'd had a rough childhood. One where she was deprived of a normal family experience.

If things worked out between them, she'd be transferring to another one. Sure, the situation was different. But would she grow to resent Jett? Or even Cooper?

The thought was a sobering one.

Yet the possibility of having to step away from this connection he had with Noel was just as painful.

"Is everything okay?" Noel had leaned across the table to put a hand on his. "I didn't mean for our conversation to get so depressing. Although, to be fair, you started it." She smiled at him, her pretty eyes shining.

"So I did." He turned his hand over so that he could hold hers. "I guess sometimes I wish life was a little less complicated." He searched for a change in topic. "So what are you doing for actual Christmas? Are you getting together with Jace and his family?"

She nodded. "I go over on Christmas Eve day. We make a ton of food and open gifts that evening, then I spend the night to see Gunner open his stocking in the morning. Grayson is too young to care about that now, but it's crazy to think there'll be two of them next year."

"That sounds like a lot of fun."

"Yeah, it is. How about you?"

"Mine is very similar. I even stay the night, too. Although Jett knows that our parents put treats in the stocking, he still gets excited." The thought of Jett waiting impatiently for everyone to get dressed and downstairs made Cooper smile. "We have a tradition where we get up way too early on Christmas morning, open stockings, and then make cinnamon rolls. We also open our gifts on Christmas Day. It's usually pretty low-key."

"Your traditions sound really nice, too. And I think it's great that Jett still gets so excited." She smiled at him, but there was a hint of something else there—a glimmer of worry or sadness.

Their food arrived then, saving them both. They talked about their favorite Christmas treats while they ate. By the time they finished, they were yawning and ready to head home.

At Noel's place, he walked her to the door and kissed her good night.

Even though he was exhausted, their conversation kept playing in his head. If there was nothing to consider except how he felt about Noel, then everything seemed straightfor-ward. He was falling in love with her—maybe he already had.

But she deserved the kind of family she'd always dreamed of. She deserved vacations on the beach and anniversary cruises. Those were things that Cooper would never be able to guarantee.

Thoughts and worries kept swirling around in his head, and it was hours before he was finally able to fall asleep.

15

By the end of the late dinner with Cooper last night, Noel couldn't shake the feeling that something had changed. He had still been kind and sweet when he dropped her off at home, but he was also different. She just couldn't quite put her finger on how.

Now, it was Saturday, and Noel had awakened early with Cooper and their conversation the night before on her mind. It seemed things had shifted once they started talking about their childhoods and what she had wanted to be when she grew up.

Had she overshared? After hearing how she'd been raised, was Cooper worried she might take a back seat when it came to her own children?

Or maybe there was nothing wrong at all, and this was her anxiety getting the best of her.

Noel sighed as she stepped out of the shower and shivered in the chilly air.

That was the problem with her anxiety. It made it difficult to determine how much she was over-stressing about something and when she really did have a reason to worry.

She dressed quickly and then used a towel to try and soak up some of the water from her hair. After she hung it back up on the hook in the bathroom, she sat down on her bed and pulled open the side table drawer. In the back right corner was the bottle of anti-anxiety medication her doctor had prescribed her four months ago.

Noel retrieved it and studied her name written on the side of the bottle.

She used to pray that she could learn to be strong enough to ignore the anxiety. That God would miraculously erase it from her life. Over time, she had come to accept that it was just part of who she was.

A part that her parents blamed her for. A part that sometimes limited what she was able to accomplish.

What if Cooper was starting to see just how much her anxiety was woven into her everyday life? He would have a lot of responsibility for caring for Jett and his many needs. He didn't need to have to add to that worrying about a wife who was going to keel over with a panic attack at the worst possible time.

In the short time she'd known Cooper, she'd already had three panic attacks in front of him. It wasn't exactly a good track record.

The sting of tears built behind her eyes. She blinked them away and threw the bottle back into the drawer.

A Country Christmas was today, and she didn't have time to wallow or deal with a headache brought on by tears.

"God, please help me to give my worries to You so that I can focus on my job today. Dull my anxiety until I'm able to ignore it." She paused in front of the bathroom mirror and looked at her reflection. She wanted to pray for Cooper. Pray for their potential relationship. But the words wouldn't come.

God knew what was in her heart. That was going to have to be good enough for now.

Noel reached for the hair dryer and finished getting ready for work.

Saturday flew by as Noel rushed around to make sure everything was in place before the event officially started at four in the afternoon. It would give people two hours of daylight to shop and enjoy the decorations and live music before the sun went down and the Christmas lights that had been displayed everywhere lit the square with their beauty.

Despite worrying that things weren't going to come together like she'd planned, the evening went off without a hitch. Everything from the horse-drawn carriage to the snow machine kept people entertained and created the perfect ambiance. Children danced beneath the falling "snow," and the scents of apple cider and cinnamon-dusted doughnuts filled the air.

The reindeer pen was a popular stop. Noel immediately thought of Jett and knew that he would've hated the crowds tonight. She was so thankful that Wyatt was able to host a much more low-key event the night before.

She wondered how things were going at the bookstore. She'd wandered past twice on her way to check on things, and it had looked busy both times.

They were most of the way through the evening when she was finally able to slow down long enough to stop by the store and say hello. Nervous energy flowed through her veins as her thoughts and worries resurfaced.

She waited for a customer to come through the door, then stepped inside. The warm air enveloped her, and only then did she realize how cold it had gotten outdoors.

Several customers milled about the store, and Cooper was taking payment from one gentleman at the counter.

As though he could sense she was there, Cooper's chin lifted, and his face lit up. He waved her in. As soon as he finished the transaction and wished his customer Merry Christmas, he turned to her.

"Hey, you," he greeted. "I hope everything has been going smoothly tonight."

"So far so good. Only little fires to put out, nothing major. How about you? Have you had some decent business?"

"It's been great. The community has been so supportive of the store. I've already got two authors who want to bring in some copies of their books for the local author display. Hopefully, word will start to spread once they do."

"That's wonderful, Cooper. I'm so happy for you."

"Thank you." He looked like he was going to reach for her but stopped himself.

Noel's stomach dropped. "Well, you put so much work into this place. You deserve for it to be a success."

"And I wouldn't be here now if it weren't for you and your help."

He was watching her, and there was something in his eyes that she didn't quite grasp. Like he had questions he was afraid to voice. Or couldn't right now.

Noel imagined he was probably seeing the same thing in her own expression.

She tried to ignore it and smiled in a way that she hoped looked normal. "Well, I had probably better get back out there. Thanks for the chance to warm up for a few minutes." She adjusted her gloves for emphasis.

"Don't let yourself get too cold," he told her. "I'll talk to you later?"

"Yeah. Good night, Cooper." With a final wave, she escaped the uncomfortable conversation and welcomed the cold air that crowded around her.

He hadn't tried to hug her, give her a kiss, or anything else.

Noel bit her bottom lip and took several deep breaths as her gaze caught on the horse-drawn carriage and the couple huddling under a blanket in the back.

The image blurred as tears gathered, and one quietly escaped to slide down her cheek.

"YOU'RE JUST GOING to have to go and talk to him." Jace's statement was so simple that it aggravated Noel.

"Thanks, Jace. I hadn't considered that." There was no missing the sarcasm in her voice. It was Sunday, and they were in the kitchen fixing pizzas at Jace and Bonnie's house.

Noel hopped up to sit on the edge of a counter. She'd told them about the odd conversation between herself and Cooper and then the even stranger interaction at the bookstore the evening before. She was hoping one of them might have some insight to put her mind at ease.

Instead, Bonnie had looked concerned, and Jace had mentioned that it was impossible to read minds. She could wonder about things until the sun set and might be stressing about certain situations or subjects that weren't even an issue.

"That's one thing I'll never understand about women," he said as he sprinkled more mozzarella cheese on the second of two pizzas. "You ladies will keep worrying about something over and over again. Create scenarios that may not even be true. You know, they say there is scientific evidence that simply going over a stressful event in your mind, even though you know it's not likely to happen, can still trigger your body to respond as though it is." He closed the cheese bag and washed his hands off in the sink. "Go talk to him, Noel, instead of borrowing trouble. He's obviously worried about something, too."

"Then why hasn't he reached out to me about it?"

Jace shrugged.

"Thanks, big brother."

He grinned at her and gave her a quick hug. "Any time. Okay, I'm going to go check on the boys. Gunner's been way too quiet for too long."

Jace left the kitchen, and Bonnie slid both pizzas into her double oven. She turned to look at Noel with sympathy. "It's not nearly as easy as Jace makes it sound. But I do think you and Cooper need to sit down and talk. Maybe you could share your concerns and see what happens after that?"

"What if I don't like the answers?"

"Then at least you'll know."

Noel groaned and ran her hands over her face. "Did Jace tell you that my doctor prescribed me some anti-anxiety medication months ago? That I decided not to take them?"

Bonnie nodded. "He mentioned it."

Noel wasn't surprised. The two of them didn't keep many secrets, and it was one of the many things about their relationship that Noel admired.

"I've been thinking about starting them—"

"He was climbing on the back of the couch—" Jace said at the same time as he came back into the kitchen. He caught what Noel was saying and stopped mid-sentence. "Sorry, I didn't mean to interrupt. Do you want me to leave?"

"No." Noel had always considered Jace to be her best friend. There was little she didn't feel comfortable talking about in front of him. "I've been considering the anti-anxiety medication again. But I just don't know if that's the answer. I know it's irrational, but the thought of being on them terrifies me."

"Then pray about it," Jace advised. "Examine the reasons for why you might take them. Is it because you want Cooper to see you differently? Because you're desperate? Or is it for you? I think if you do that, you'll come to the right conclusion."

Noel shifted to sit cross-legged on the counter. "And you have no official opinion?"

"I've told you, little sister. Do what *you* need. What's right for *you*. Don't let what our parents might say influence you, and don't let your fear of losing Cooper affect your decision." He shrugged. "I'm here for you. Always. To listen. To give advice. But this is something you have to decide for yourself. Just know that no matter what you decide, we're both here for you."

Noel hopped down from the counter and immediately found herself being hugged by both of them. "I love you guys."

"We love you, too."

The oven timer went off, and Jace pulled back with a clap of his hands. "Okay," he hollered as he directed his voice in the direction of the living room. "Who's ready for some pizza and a Disney movie?"

"Meeeee!!" The little voice yelled back, followed by thundering footsteps as Gunner raced into the room.

Grayson started fussing then, and Bonnie lifted one eyebrow at Jace.

"Sorry. Although he was going to be waking up any minute now anyway."

Bonnie's stern look melted away. "I'll go feed the little guy if you'll get everything else ready. I'll meet you guys in there shortly."

Noel watched as Jace got Gunner a piece of pizza, but her mind was on the earlier conversation.

Bonnie was right. Noel needed to talk to Cooper. Because as much as she dreaded the answer he might give her, not knowing was even worse.

16

The last thing Cooper wanted to do was break up with Noel. Was it even breaking up if they hadn't put an official title on their relationship yet? Well, that's what it felt like he was considering. He could tell Noel sensed things were off Saturday night when she stopped by the store. Maybe she was overwhelmed with the event and everything she had to keep track of, but he didn't think so.

She'd seemed distracted. Concerned.

And he'd felt like a heel for distancing himself a little then, too.

With the exception of a handful of relatively generic texts between Sunday and Monday, it was clear neither of them was willing to break the silence.

Which was why they needed to talk. They couldn't keep going like this. At least he couldn't, anyway. He wanted to see what she was thinking. See what concerns she might have about their relationship and whether a future together was even possible.

But right now, he needed to get through his Tuesday. A workday that had turned out to be an odd one. Jett's day classes had been canceled because there were too many teachers out sick. So Cooper had brought him in with him since his parents had several doctors' appointments they'd already scheduled for the day.

Jett normally enjoyed being at the bookstore. But since his day had been thrown off schedule and everything was different, he'd had a difficult time settling down.

He'd asked for Noel a handful of times, requested to go home more times than Cooper could count, and was generally requiring a great deal of supervision and redirection.

Cooper answered a question about reindeer for the fifth time and then prayed for an extra dose of patience.

It was fifteen minutes after five. At least he and Jett could eat the packed dinner he'd brought soon. That would buy him a half hour or so. Jett just needed to last until eight, and then Cooper would happily close the bookstore and take his brother home.

His phone rang, and he glanced at the screen before answering it. "Hey, Dad."

"Cooper? Your mom and I were in a car accident. We're okay, but I'm pretty sure the car is totaled. Your mom hit her head in the impact, so we're going to the hospital to have her checked out. It's just a precaution."

Alarm coursed through Cooper's veins. "What? That doesn't sound like she's okay to me. Which hospital are you going to?"

"Clearwater General. You don't need to come in—you know how Jett does with doctors. I'll call you as soon as we get the all clear. I've got to go."

"All right. Love you guys."

"Love you, too, son."

The call ended, and nervous energy set in. Cooper had paced back and forth between the front counter and the main office three times before chimes brought his attention to the door.

Noel breezed in, a hesitant smile on her face. She must have seen the concern on his face because her eyes immediately narrowed. "What's wrong?"

He lowered his voice and told her about the call, being careful not to alarm Jett.

"You should go check on them."

"I can't. Jett doesn't do well at hospitals, and it'll cause more stress that they don't need right now."

Noel put a hand on his arm, and the gesture brought his gaze back to hers. "I'll stay here with Jett. We'll be fine. Go check on them."

Cooper didn't think it was a good idea. She'd never been left alone with Jett before. Then again, she could feed Jett dinner, and Cooper could check on his parents and be back again as soon as he saw that they were okay.

She must have sensed his hesitation. "What do I need to do?"

"Okay," he said, having made his decision to go. "Dinner is packed in the cooler in the office. Jett's been a little out of sorts since he should be home right now to start with. And if you need to, just close the store early. I don't want you to have to deal with everything." He turned to Jett. "Hey, buddy. Come here for a second." He placed a palm against his brother's chest. "Noel is going to stay with you for a little while tonight. I need to run an errand, but I'll be back real soon. Can you help Noel if she needs it?"

Jett looked from Cooper to Noel and then back again. "Where you going?"

"I need to take care of a few things. But I will be back soon. You make sure you listen to Noel. Okay?"

Jett nodded slowly. "Okay."

He reached over and gave Noel's hand a squeeze, then handed her a key. "That way you can lock up the store if you need to. You call me about anything. I'm serious."

"I will."

"Thank you, Noel." Before he changed his mind, he grabbed his coat and darted out of the bookstore.

"I DON'T LIKE it when Cooper leaves."

It was the third time Jett had told Noel as much. He'd been walking from the children's section to the front, his eye on the door as though he expected his brother to come right back.

She'd tried to distract him by talking about Rudy, but that didn't help.

Then she remembered the cooler. "Let's get your dinner. Are you hungry? I'll bet Rudy is starving."

Jett stopped pacing. "Eat dinner and then find Cooper?"

"Well, we definitely need to eat before we do anything else. When our stomach isn't hungry, it makes it a lot easier to think about everything else."

Jett seemed to consider what she said and finally nodded his agreement. He followed her into the office, where she set him up at the desk. Inside the cooler, she found a sandwich, chips, a bottle of juice, and a package of cookies. She got all of that out for Jett and breathed a sigh of relief when he finally focused on his meal.

Noel gave his shoulder a gentle squeeze. "I'm going to go up front and watch for customers."

"And Cooper."

"Yes, and I'll watch for Cooper, too."

She made sure he was going to stay and eat, then went to

stand by the front counter. She glanced at her phone, not that she expected a text from Cooper yet.

Not knowing what was going on was the worst, which is why it was so important for Cooper to go and check on his parents. "Father, please put Your arms around Mr. and Mrs. Meyer," she whispered. "Guide the hands of the doctors as they care for them and help them to be okay."

Two different customers came into the store while Jett was eating. She helped one with a purchase and wished the other a good evening when she left empty-handed.

Jett came out into the main area then with his empty paper plate in his hands. "I'm full."

"Wow, you did eat well. Nicely done." She took the plate from him and threw it away. "Do you want to play a game? Or look at the Christmas hidden picture book? Did you bring that in with you today?"

Noel thought he was going to say no, but he retrieved the book from a backpack behind the counter and presented it to her.

They went through the book, found the reindeer on every page, and talked about the theme of each of the scenes. In one, all the buildings were made out of gingerbread. In another, everything was ice and snow.

A half-hour later, Jett had lost interest in the book and was back to walking around with Rudy clutched under one arm.

What would happen if Cooper wasn't back before eight? Should she close the store but stay here with Jett? Or take Jett to her house? She could take him home and wait with him there, but she had no way to get inside.

At that point, maybe she should take him to the hospital, too. All she knew was that Jett didn't handle that kind of situation well, and she didn't feel comfortable taking Jett there without knowing all the details.

Noel breathed in deeply and pushed away the nerves and what-ifs that were starting to clamor for attention.

Worst case scenario, she could call Wyatt for backup. He'd know what to do in a situation like this.

"We can go look for Cooper," Jett announced and pointed to the door.

As calmly as she could, Noel stepped between him and the door. "I think we should wait here. Let's go look at the books. I'm sure we can find one you haven't seen yet."

She started to lead the way to the children's section when a blood-curdling scream sounded from behind her. It sent her heart into overdrive, and the hair on the back of her neck stood on end.

She whirled to find Jett standing where she'd left him, eyes wide and a look of horror on his face.

A woman had come into the store with a young girl. In the girl's arms was a very realistic-looking horse. The poor girl was staring at Jett, fear in her eyes.

In the blink of an eye, the little girl began to cry and dropped her horse as she turned to her mom for comfort.

Jett saw that the horse was no longer being held, screamed again, and ran for the door leading outside. With a quick push against the door, he disappeared.

"Jett! Stop!"

Noel's breath caught in her throat, and she coughed. She turned to the customer. "I'm so sorry. He's scared of horses. He has severe special needs. I need to close the store and find him."

"Of course." The woman uttered several apologies as she picked up the dropped horse and hurried her daughter out of the store.

Noel felt horrible for turning the woman away, but she

didn't have time to placate a potential customer. She had to find Jett.

She exited the store, turned to lock it, and took in the street and sidewalk outside. It was getting dark, which made it difficult to see faces well in the twilight. A cold breeze whipped past, and Noel realized she'd left her coat inside. So had Jett.

"Jett! Come back! The horse is gone!"

Nothing.

A band began to tighten around her chest as blood pounded in her ears. She tried to catch her breath. A guttural groan escaped her throat in anger. She was mad at herself for not stopping Jett before he got out of the store. She was furious at herself for going into panic attack mode when she needed to find him. But most of all, she was devastated because Cooper had trusted her with Jett's care, and she'd failed.

Did Jett know anything about traffic safety? Did he know how to ask someone for help if he was lost?

The band grew tighter as tears formed in her eyes.

"Please, God. I need to find him."

She swallowed hard, straightened, and pushed forward. She ignored the burning sensation in her chest and asked someone on the sidewalk if he'd seen a young man with a reindeer plush.

The third person she met pointed across the street and down.

Noel thanked her and jogged across the street. "Jett!"

Determination flooded in, forcing the panic to recede.

She stopped in the middle of the sidewalk and did a half turn, praying she'd catch sight of Jett. She was about ready to jog further down the street when the lighted plane hanging above Mr. Brooks' store caught her eye.

Going on pure instinct, she ran to the store and pulled the door open. "Mr. Brooks! Have you seen—"

She stopped short when she spotted Mr. Brooks trying to show Jett an expansive marble run that was set up near the front counter. But Jett just clutched Rudy, his eyes wide. "I need Cooper. Where is Cooper?"

Noel nearly sagged with relief. She rushed forward. "Jett. There you are. I was worried about you."

Jett turned to look at her, a frown on his face. "Horses are scary."

"I know." She put an arm around his shoulders. "The horse is gone. I promise it's not in the store anymore. Can we go back?"

Jett shook his head and sat on the floor for emphasis.

Mr. Brooks gave her a sympathetic look and waved her over. "He came in maybe ten minutes ago. He was obviously scared, but I couldn't get any information about who he was other than his first name and his brother's first name. I figured someone would be looking for him. I would've called the police in another fifteen minutes otherwise." He nodded toward Jett. "I take it he's with you?"

Jett held Rudy close and rocked back and forth on the floor.

"His brother had a family emergency. I was watching him at the bookstore. Clearly, I did a horrible job of it." She couldn't keep the catch out of her voice. "If he hadn't come in here. If I hadn't found him…"

"But you did." Mr. Brooks put a kind hand on her arm, something that would've taken her by surprise if she wasn't still running off fear and adrenaline. "And he's okay."

Noel nodded as she tried to calm her racing heart. Yes, Jett was okay. Although, he was clearly still terrified. "Thank you for being here for him."

For the first time, Mr. Brooks gave her a small, encouraging smile.

She went to sit cross-legged in front of Jett, who was shaking. "Hey. I know that horse was really scary. I'm so sorry that it snuck up on you like that. But I made sure the little girl took the horse and left the store."

Jett shook his head back and forth, his breath coming in short gasps.

"I need you to focus, Jett. I need you to take slow breaths in and out. Look at Rudy. What color is his nose?"

Jett touched it with the tip of his finger. "Black," he said between gasps.

"Good! And look at the blanket he has. It's so colorful. And I'll bet it's keeping him warm. I think I like the red in the blanket best. Do you like red or green?"

The younger man's breathing slowed as he processed her question. "Red, too."

"We like the same color. I knew it!" She smiled at him and prayed that she could get him calm enough to get him back to the bookstore.

17

The radio in Cooper's car belted out Christmas music as he drove back to the square and the bookstore. Thankfully, his mom was okay. There was no evidence of a concussion or any other damage to her head. Considering the condition of his parents' vehicle, it was a miracle that neither of them was hurt.

He had to squelch the anger that boiled to the surface when he thought about the drunk driver who had run a red light and slammed right into them. His parents could've been killed. The very thought had him gripping the steering wheel tight enough to turn his knuckles white.

As it was, the driver was lucky that everyone had walked away from the accident.

He'd waited for his parents to make a police report, then dropped them off at home. He planned to get Jett, close the store early, and then spend the night at their house just in case they needed anything.

It wasn't a total surprise when he walked up to the bookstore and found it closed. He'd told Noel she could close early if she needed to. But when he knocked on the door with no response, he started to get worried. A quick glance around the area revealed no sign of Noel or Jett.

He pulled his phone out and texted,

"Where are you?"

It was nearly a full five minutes later before he finally got an answer.

"Mr. Brooks' Collectibles."

By then, he was not only worried but frustrated. If she'd needed to take Jett somewhere else, she should have texted and let Cooper know.

He ran down the street and across to the collectibles store. He burst through the door to find Noel helping Jett get up off the floor. "What on earth happened?"

When Noel turned, her expression was a mix of sadness and apprehension.

Jett ran to Cooper for a hug. "I got lost."

A man who must be Mr. Brooks stepped forward. "From what we can gather, he came in here almost immediately. Less than ten minutes later, Noel came looking for him."

Cooper tried to digest the information. "You lost Jett for over ten minutes? It's cold and getting dark, Noel. What if he'd crossed the road when a car was coming?" His words came out much harsher than he'd intended as anger toward the drunk driver redirected itself at her.

She flinched, and guilt stabbed him in the heart.

"I'm sorry," Noel began. "I turned my back for a second. There was a horse toy, and the next thing I knew, Jett was gone." She pulled the store key out of her pocket and handed it to him. "I ran right after him, but I didn't see where he went."

Cooper struggled to put all the pieces together. He held his brother close and patted him on the back. "It's okay, buddy. It's okay." What horse toy was Noel talking about? He'd certainly seen Jett freak out over a horse. But for him to get away completely…

If he'd been there for his brother like he was supposed to be, none of this would've happened. He should've taken Jett to the hospital and dealt with whatever might have happened there. Or stayed at the store and waited for news from Dad. "I never should have left him."

"I hope your parents are okay, Cooper. I'm truly sorry."

With a last look at Jett, Noel exited the store. He hated for her to leave like that, but he needed to deal with Jett right now and get back to the house.

Mr. Brooks gave Cooper a look of disapproval. "She was beside herself when she came in looking for your brother."

She probably should have been, but he kept the comment to himself. Instead, Cooper stuck out a hand. "Thank you for watching after him until she came in. I appreciate it."

Mr. Brooks shook it. "Of course."

"Come on, buddy. Let's go get your coat and go home."

Back at the store, he grabbed the cooler and Jett's things, and then spotted Noel's coat draped over the chair in the office. He took that, too, and they made their way to his car.

"We're going to drop this off for Noel before we head home," he told Jett. When he parked in front of her house, he faced his brother. "Stay right here. I'll be back in a minute." He turned the engine off and jogged to her front door.

It took nearly a full minute after he knocked for her to open the door. Her eyes were red-rimmed, and it was clear she'd been crying. The sight made his heart hurt. "You left this at the store," he said kindly as he held the coat out. "It's too cold to be walking around without it."

She took it and gave a slight nod. "Thanks." She brushed some of her hair off her face. "Look, Cooper. I don't know if…" she faltered.

"…if this is going to work out between us," he finished, his voice sounding monotone to his own ears.

"I'm sorry, Cooper. For everything."

"Me, too, Noel." How could this be happening? As though his limbs were made of wood, he motioned to the car. "I need to get Jett back to the house. Good night."

"Good night."

He heard her door shut softly behind him as he walked away.

NOEL TOOK a sip of her hot cocoa and accepted a roll of scotch tape from Jace. "Thank you." After setting the mug on the coffee table, she used the tape to secure one side of a Christmas gift she was wrapping.

A couple of years ago, Jace and Bonnie had invited her over for cocoa and gift wrapping, followed by a Christmas movie. They'd been doing it ever since. Noel loved to show her brother and sister-in-law the gifts she'd gotten for the boys and see what all they'd chosen as well.

It was hard to believe that Christmas was only a few days away.

It'd been a long few weeks since the incident with Jett. The only time Noel had seen Cooper was from afar, and neither of them had tried texting or calling the other.

And she missed him. Desperately.

With Christmas coming up, there were a lot of distractions to help keep her busy. She didn't look forward to the lonely days that were coming after that.

Noel pulled another toy out of the large canvas bag she brought.

Jace took it from her. "What is this?"

"I got it for Grayson. It makes a noise as he pushes it around on the floor. It's supposed to promote crawling."

Jace gave it a try, and the resulting sound was so loud that Bonnie and Noel shushed him simultaneously.

He gave Noel an amused look. "Please don't take it personally if the batteries never get replaced once they die."

Noel laughed out loud. "I'll try not to." With that, she started wrapping the gift.

There'd been something she wanted to tell them both, but Jace especially, and she'd been working up the courage for nearly two weeks now. This seemed like as good of a time as any.

She set the toy down on the floor, the wrapping only half finished.

"I've been taking anti-anxiety medication for almost two weeks now."

The announcement silenced the room. Jace blinked at her. "Are you serious?"

"Yeah. I figured it was about time." She held up a hand to stop her brother because she knew what he was going to say next. "It wasn't about what happened with Jett. It didn't have anything to do with Cooper or Mom and Dad. I'd been thinking and praying about what you told me, Jace, about doing what was best for me. I decided I was tired of not feeling in control. So one night, I got the medication bottle out and popped it open for the first time. I figured I wouldn't know if I didn't try. Right?"

Bonnie reached over and rested a hand on Noel's arm. "How are you feeling? Has it helped?"

"The first few days, I felt so sick to my stomach I barely noticed anything else. But once I got used to it … yeah. It's helped. A lot." They were the first people she'd told, and being able to get that off her chest was such a huge relief. She gave a little laugh as tears gathered in her eyes. "I've always felt the way I did. I didn't realize it could be different. I…" the words lodged in her throat.

Jace scooted over and put his arms around her. "I'm proud of you, Noel."

Bonnie gave her a hug from the other side. "It was a brave thing to do."

For several minutes, Noel let the tears fall as she soaked in the love around her. Finally, she swiped at her cheeks, and when the others leaned back, she discovered their eyes were suspiciously watery as well.

"Now that I know I can feel like this, I don't ever want to go back." She let out a shaky laugh. "I wish I'd started taking it sooner. Why didn't I?" She'd asked herself that question over and over again over the last two weeks.

If her parents had taken her to a doctor to address her anxiety instead of ridiculing her for it, Noel wondered how different her life might have been.

"You weren't ready," Jace said simply. "And there's nothing wrong with that."

They went back to wrapping the gifts they'd forgotten earlier.

"Are you going to keep your job after all?" Bonnie asked.

"No. I'm not sure what I'm going to do next." Truthfully, she was just trying to get through the next few weeks working downtown and wondering whether she was going to run into Cooper. Part of her wanted to. She felt like there were a lot of things that needed to be said. But another part of her thought it would be easier once she was working somewhere else. Somewhere not on the town square.

"You're always welcome to move onto the farm," Jace told her, and Bonnie echoed her agreement.

"I know. And you guys are great. But I'm happy in my house for now. I'm considering talking to Wyatt and seeing if they ever need full-time help at the stables."

Bonnie smiled at the suggestion. "That would be perfect. They'd be lucky to have you."

There were a few moments filled with nothing but the sounds of scissors working and the tearing of tape.

Finally, Jace asked, "Nothing from Cooper?"

"Nope. But it's not like I've texted him, either."

Jace hadn't had a problem telling her he thought that Cooper had been a fool to walk away. Right now, he stayed silent.

Noel's eyes narrowed. "You think I should. Reach out."

He shrugged. "All I know is that regrets are difficult to live with."

She glanced at one of the bags of gifts she'd brought in. It held items she'd bought for Cooper and Jett the day before everything fell apart. She had considered taking them and returning them, but never could quite make herself.

Regardless of how things were now, the gifts were bought for Cooper and Jett, and Noel couldn't imagine doing anything else with them. So she'd wrap them and take them by tomorrow.

At least then, they wouldn't be sitting around as a constant reminder of what might have been.

THE LAST FEW weeks since the car accident and the episode with Jett had been busy ones, and yet the time seemed to drag. Cooper was thankful he'd hired people to work for him at the bookstore, and one employee seemed to fit in especially well. After the new year, he hoped Ron might be interested in training for a managerial position. It'd be nice to be able to step away from the store occasionally and know it was in good hands.

Cooper's gaze swept over the store to make sure no one needed assistance, and his gaze caught on the Charlotte's Web poster. His heart ached as nearly everything reminded him of Noel, including the axolotls on display near the counter and even the sound of the chimes when people entered the building.

For a while, he'd half expected her to come walking through that door every time he heard them.

He missed her more than he ever thought possible.

Jett did, too. He asked about Noel on a regular basis. Cooper didn't have the heart to say that they might not see her again. He was having a hard time accepting that possibility himself.

Tomorrow was Friday, and he looked forward to working that one last day and then having three days off for Christmas. It'd be great to have a chance to recover from the craziness that the last month had brought. But the store was doing well, and Cooper couldn't be more pleased with that progress.

The chimes rang out, and Mr. Brooks walked into the store.

"Merry Christmas," Cooper greeted and shook the older man's hand.

Mr. Brooks only nodded his reply. He held out a memory card. "It's the security footage from the night your brother found his way to my store. I wanted to get it to you before, but it's all digital and kept up on the cloud somewhere. My grandson is in town for Christmas, and he was able to download it for me yesterday."

Cooper couldn't have been more surprised as he accepted the tiny SD card. "Thank you, sir."

"You're welcome." Mr. Brooks looked around the store. "You've got a real nice place here. Merry Christmas."

With that, he was gone again.

Cooper stared at the memory card that rested in the palm of his hand.

He retrieved his laptop from the office. After the night when Jett ran away, Cooper had pulled the security footage from the lone camera in his store. Sure enough, a woman and her daughter had come into the store with a toy horse. From the looks of it, Jett had been giving Noel a run for her money before he took off. Based on her position in relation to the door, he wasn't sure Noel could've prevented Jett from escaping.

He'd been harsh with Noel. He realized that and regretted it deeply. But she'd been clear that she didn't think their relationship could work. How could he blame her? He'd left her with Jett on a day his brother was struggling anyway. It would make anyone second-guess a decision that might leave her caring for someone with severe special needs.

As much as it hurt to admit it, he wasn't sure he could give her what she needed in a relationship, either. At least not when it came to their family and quality time together. She deserved those family vacations and trips she dreamed about.

So he'd kept his distance. And every day, he wondered if he was doing the right thing.

With a heavy sigh, he slipped the SD card into the computer and pulled up the footage.

It broke his heart to see Jett stumbling into the collectibles store, crying and upset. Mr. Brooks had tried to distract him, but Jett would have none of it.

Then Jett showed signs of having a panic attack until Noel sat on the floor with him and talked him through it. She got him to calm down.

Jett had finally agreed to go with her back to the store when Cooper had burst in.

For his younger brother to go back to a place where a horse scared him was huge and spoke of Jett's trust in Noel.

Regret settled in his chest as he watched the footage one more time.

He understood why Noel might want to step away from their relationship. He would respect that. But she deserved to know that he didn't blame her for what happened to Jett that night, and it was something he shouldn't have put off like he did.

18

I t had taken Noel all Friday morning to get up the nerve to walk down to the bookstore and talk to Cooper. When her lunch hour rolled around, she really didn't have any more excuses. She reached for the bag she'd stashed under her desk and headed out with a steadying breath.

Honestly, she had no idea what to expect. Would the Christmas gifts break the ice? Or would he refuse to even take them?

Noel frowned and did her best to squelch the nerves that were making her stomach hurt.

But when she walked through the bookstore door and the chimes announced her arrival, there was no sign of Cooper at all. Instead, a man in his late twenties stood behind the main counter. He gave her a bright smile.

"Merry Christmas! Is there anything I can help you find?"

Her eyes darted to his name tag. This must be one of the people Cooper had said he'd hired.

Pushing down her disappointment, she returned the smile. "Hi, Ron. I was looking for Cooper. Is he in today?"

"He was, but he left for lunch about ten minutes ago.

He'll be back before one." Ron pulled a piece of paper and pen out from behind the counter. "You're welcome to come back. Or would you like to leave a message?"

Noel almost declined, but it'd taken a lot to convince herself to come this time. She wasn't sure if she could make a second trip later in the day. The weight of the bag on her shoulder reminded her that she was there to leave the gifts, and she could do that whether Cooper was there or not. "That would be great, thank you."

She took the pen from him and wrote a note that she slid into the bag. "I would appreciate it if you could make sure he gets this." Reluctantly, she handed the bag with the gifts over to Ron.

"I sure will."

"Thank you. Have a blessed Christmas."

"You as well!"

Noel turned and walked out of the store, but it felt like a little piece of her heart stayed behind.

***

COOPER WELCOMED the warmth of the bookstore as he and Jett entered after getting lunch together. Since it was nearly Christmas, Cooper thought it would be fun to get hamburgers and fries instead of taking their usual sandwiches.

He handed a bag to Ron, who had covered the store while they were gone. "Here you go. A burger with the works and fries as requested."

"Thanks, boss," Ron said as he took the bag. "I've been looking forward to this. Oh! A woman stopped by while you were gone and dropped something off. I put it on the chair in the office."

"Awesome, thank you. Thanks for all your hard work

over the last couple of weeks. I hope you have a wonderful Christmas."

"Merry Christmas to you, too. See you next week!" Ron gave a wave and hurried from the store. Cooper had sent him home early to start his holiday vacation.

Jett took his coat off and stuffed it into a basket behind the counter. "It's cold outside."

"It sure is, buddy. What do you want to do now?"

Jett didn't respond, but he did pick up his backpack and take it to the bean bag chair, where he promptly sat down.

Cooper went into the office and brought the large canvas bag back to the main part of the store, where he could keep an eye on Jett.

Inside were two wrapped gifts and a folded piece of paper. He retrieved the paper and read,

Cooper, I bought these for you and Jett weeks ago, and I wanted to make sure you got them. I'm sorry I missed you. Please tell Jett I said hello. Merry Christmas. - Noel

He touched her name as disappointment over having missed her hit hard. He pulled a large, thin package out of the bag and spotted his name written in Noel's handwriting. The other package was more the size of a shoebox with Jett's name written on a gift tag in one corner.

"Hey, Jett. Noel brought a Christmas present by for you."

Jett completely forgot about his backpack and everything in it as he ran across the store. Cooper handed him the package and watched as his brother made quick work of the wrapping paper. Cooper helped him open the plain box inside to reveal a reindeer puzzle and a reindeer-themed board game. "Reindeer, Cooper! Noel got reindeer!" He clapped his hands and took it all with him to the bean bag chair.

Noel couldn't have chosen a better gift for him.

Curious about what his own present contained, Cooper

unwrapped it and gasped. It was a framed map of Middle Earth from *The Hobbit*.

It was perfect, and the fact that she remembered their conversation about their favorite books from weeks ago meant a lot to him. Especially given the gift he'd chosen for her, which was wrapped and waiting in the office. Once again, Cooper wished he'd been there when she came by. He could've given the gift to her then and seen her face when she opened it.

Cooper parked near the large ranch house and hoped the family didn't mind if he dropped by. It wasn't hard to track down the address. There was no denying he was nervous, but he had to talk to Noel. He should have talked to her days ago.

With a prayer for peace and guidance, he retrieved a bag from the back seat and headed for the front door.

The sounds of a little boy laughing inside brought a smile to his face as he rang the doorbell.

Moments later, the door swung open, and Jace's eyebrows rose in surprise. "Cooper. I must admit I'm surprised to see you. Merry Christmas."

Cooper took the offered hand and shook it. "Merry Christmas. I like the shirt."

Jace tugged on the bottom of his Dallas Cowboys sweatshirt. "Thanks. It's a Christmas gift from my wife," he said with a smile. "Would you like to come in?"

"If it won't be an imposition. I won't stay long."

Jace stepped to the side and motioned for him to enter, then closed the door again behind them.

Cooper took in the simple yet elegant décor. "You have a beautiful home."

"Thank you. My grandfather designed and built it many years ago." He motioned to a doorway on the other side of the room. "Everyone else is through here if you'll follow me."

The moment Cooper stepped through the doorway, his gaze landed on Noel. She was sitting on the couch next to Bonnie. She looked comfortable in sweatpants, a baggy Christmas shirt, and her hair pulled up in a messy bun that threatened to tumble at any moment. But it was the baby in her arms that snagged his attention the most. His face was nestled against her neck as she slowly rubbed his back.

Her eyes widened when she saw him.

"Merry Christmas, everyone. I'm sorry to intrude." Cooper smiled at the little boy playing on the floor. He reached inside the bag he was carrying and pulled out a square container. "I brought homemade cinnamon rolls. They are my mom's specialty that she makes every Christmas." He handed the container to Jace, who took it appreciatively.

"They look amazing. Thank you." Jace glanced at Noel, and something passed between the twins that Cooper was unable to decipher.

"I'm sure we'll enjoy the cinnamon rolls," Noel said as she stood with the baby. "Please thank your mom for us." She gently swayed with the baby.

There was something about seeing her there, an infant in her arms, that had Cooper's mind going down a path that he had no right to hope for.

The little boy on the floor hopped up and stood in front of Cooper. "Hi! I'm Gunner. Do you want to see what Auntie got me for Christmas?" Without waiting for an answer, he presented a transforming robot. "See? He can change into a tank!"

Cooper crouched down and watched as Gunner demonstrated the robot's abilities.

"Wow, that's one of the coolest robot tanks I've ever seen," he said with an encouraging smile. "That aunt of yours definitely picked a good toy."

Gunner turned and grinned at Noel. "She sure did!"

Cooper chuckled and stood up again. He cleared his throat and pressed the palm of one hand against the back of his neck. He looked at Noel. "Would it be okay if we talked for a few minutes?"

She nodded and turned to hand the baby to Bonnie. Noel smoothed the front of her shirt and stepped around several toys on the floor until she was standing in front of him.

Jace scooped Gunner into his arms. "Let's go take these cinnamon rolls into the kitchen and get some chocolate milk. How does that sound?"

"Awesome!"

Bonnie followed her husband. Cooper didn't miss the encouraging look that she gave her sister-in-law.

When the rest of the family was gone, Cooper took in every detail about Noel. He'd missed everything from her beautiful blue eyes to the way she was clasping her hands together in front of her.

"Jett and I got the gifts you left. I'm sorry we weren't there when you came by."

"That's okay. I'm just glad you got them. I hope Jett liked his. When I saw them, I couldn't say no." Her eyes sparkled as she spoke.

"The puzzle and game were a huge hit." He paused. "And the picture was amazing, Noel. Thank you for not only remembering what my favorite book is, but finding something so fun and unique. I've already got it hanging up in the store." He reached into the bag and pulled out a present wrapped in red paper. "This is for you. I bought this a few weeks ago, too."

Noel reached for the gift and carefully removed the bow before she peeled the wrapping away to reveal a large book. She gasped when she turned it over in her hands and saw the cover. "Anne of Green Gables. It looks just like the one my grandma gave me." Tears flooded her eyes.

Cooper nodded. "I remember you told me she gave it to you when you were ten. So I researched which copies were being printed at that time and hoped it was the right one."

She clutched it to her chest. "Thank you. It's perfect," she said, her voice just above a whisper.

"You're welcome." He desperately wanted to reach out to her. Instead, he motioned to the couch. "Do you mind if we sit down?"

She claimed a spot on the couch, and he followed suit. Before he had a chance to say anything, Noel took in a steadying breath. "I should have come back by the store and apologized for what happened. I was responsible for Jett, and I—"

Cooper held up a hand to stop her. "I'm the one who should apologize. I was angry before I even knew Jett was missing, and I'm afraid I took it out on the situation. On you." He told her about the drunk driver who had plowed into his parents' car. "On top of that, Jett had been having a rough day, and I knew that. I never should have left him. Not because I didn't trust you, but because I knew that Jett would need more help than normal, and that was my responsibility." He paused. "Instead, I left everything for you to handle. And that wasn't fair. I'm sorry, Noel."

"I'm sure knowing some of that would have helped. But the fact is, I was responsible for Jett at that point in time, and because I wasn't paying enough attention, he could have gotten lost or hurt. I didn't have control of the situation." She swallowed hard. "That was on me."

"Mr. Brooks brought me an early Christmas present yesterday." That brought a shocked look to Noel's face, and Cooper chuckled at her reaction. "I was pretty surprised myself. He had downloaded the store footage of that night when Jett ran into his store." He shifted so that he was facing her on the couch. "Noel, you may have lost Jett, but you tracked him down. You didn't give up. Not only did you find him, but you talked him down from a panic attack, and then you convinced him to return to the bookstore before I even got there. You didn't just regain control of the situation, but you handled it like a boss."

Noel let out a shaky breath. "Thank you." She visibly relaxed, and instead of sitting straight on the couch, she leaned into the back. "I hope you realize that you're an amazing brother to Jett. And that the level of protectiveness you showed when you couldn't find him was warranted. I should have texted you right away when he ran out of the store."

Her words meant a great deal to him. "I appreciate that," he said, his voice sounding deeper than normal.

They were both silent for several heartbeats until they spoke at the same time.

"I've missed you."

"I've missed you, Noel."

They both laughed, and some of the tension seemed to dissipate.

There were a lot of things Cooper wanted to say to her. He ran a hand over his goatee as he searched for the right words. "I know my situation is a lot. I respect your need to step away from it. But I value your friendship, Noel, and I don't want to lose that." He reached into the bag again and pulled out the last item hiding at the bottom. He lifted the black axolotl with a flourish. "I think of you every time I see this guy, so I thought you should have it. Truthfully? I think he's missed you, too."

Noel accepted the plush and fingered the little T-shirt it wore. "Thank you." Her long eyelashes lifted as her gaze met his. She held the axolotl to her chest. "I value your friendship, too. And for what it's worth, I never saw your situation with Jett as too much. If anything, it says a lot about the kind of man you are. There is no doubt in my mind that you would take care of your own family and love them fiercely. But I understood that you might feel as though you can't trust me. With Jett." It was clear she was referring to more than just his brother. "Between my anxiety issues and the way I was raised, you'd have every reason to be concerned about what kind of a mother figure I might turn out to be. You're already responsible for Jett. The last thing you needed was having to help someone else through regular panic attacks."

Cooper's eyes widened. "That's what you thought?" He leaned forward and reached for her hand, holding it gently in his. "I felt for you and your anxiety, but I never saw it as a burden. I think dealing with it like you have has given you a deep empathy for others who might be going through some-thing that most people can't see or understand. It's what helped you connect with Jett the way you did." He ran his thumb over her knuckles. "I wouldn't hesitate to trust you with Jett again. I'm proud of who you are, Noel." A stray tear started to slide down her cheek, and Cooper reached up to wipe it away with the pad of his thumb. "Sweetheart, I need you in my life."

Noel took in a steadying breath. "I'm glad because I need you, too. I love you, Cooper."

"And I am so in love with you." He shifted closer and slowly studied every inch of her face before gathering her in his arms and kissing her.

EPILOGUE

MAY - FIVE MONTHS LATER

Noel studied herself in the mirror. The wedding dress she'd chosen fit her perfectly, with lacy sleeves covering her arms. Mrs. Meyer, who insisted that Noel call her Rachel, had helped her get dressed. Then Bonnie had used a pretty clasp to bring part of Noel's hair up and curled it so that it twisted and fell down her back.

A knock drew her attention to the door. Jace peeked in and smiled. "Mind if I come in? I think they're about ready for you down there."

Bonnie motioned for him to come inside, then she turned and gave Noel a gentle hug. "I'm so happy for you. We'll see you in a few minutes, okay?"

Noel nodded, then accepted a hug from Rachel as well.

They closed the door behind them, leaving Noel and Jace alone.

"You look amazing, Noel. Cooper's jaw is going to drop."

"You really think so?" Noel grinned.

"Most definitely."

Noel's smile faltered a bit. "Are they down there?"

"No. They didn't come."

She'd officially invited their parents to the wedding and had made it clear that they were to be guests only and to keep things civil. She shouldn't be surprised that they'd chosen not to come. Even more, she should be relieved. It still stung, though.

Jace nudged her with his elbow. "Come on, I've got your back. Just like always, right?" He smiled at her.

Noel forcibly pushed thoughts of their parents away and smiled back at him. "That's right, big brother." One of the first things Noel did after she and Cooper were officially engaged was to ask Jace if he would walk her down the aisle. He'd immediately accepted.

He held an arm out to her. "Shall we go?"

Noel slipped her hand through his arm and gave it a squeeze. "Let's do it."

"Cooper is a lucky man, and don't you let him forget it. I'll always be here if he needs a reminder."

She chuckled. "I know you will, Jace, and I appreciate it."

He escorted her into the foyer of the church and to the worship hall where the wedding was taking place. A set of double doors had been propped open, and music welcomed them in.

As they started down the aisle, Noel immediately sought out Cooper. Seeing him standing at the end waiting for her stilled any remaining nerves.

Next to Cooper stood Jett, who he'd asked to be his best man, and his dad. David Meyer had to gently help Jett stay in place when he saw her and started to wave. Noel smiled and waved back at him.

Cooper caught her gaze then and held it as she and Jace drew closer. They stopped in front of the pastor, and Noel turned and handed her bouquet to Bonnie, who was serving as her matron of honor. Jace kissed Noel's cheek before placing her hand in Cooper's.

"Sweetheart, you are gorgeous," Cooper whispered in her ear.

He gently squeezed her hand and then never let it go until the ceremony was complete and they were introduced as Mr. and Mrs. Cooper Meyer.

Cooper gently pulled her into his arms. His lips found hers in a kiss that didn't just express his joy and love. It promised forever.

———

THANK you so much for reading *Marrying Noel*. I hope you enjoyed the final book in the Brides of Clearwater series. This has been such a special series to write, and I hope it's been a blessing to you.

If you're looking for another series to read, I suggest you check out Danger in Destiny. *Out of the Ashes* is the first book in this Christian romantic suspense series.

He thought it was just a structure fire.

AS A FIREFIGHTER, Bryce Keyes is no stranger when it comes to running into a burning building. What he didn't expect was coming face-to-face with the woman he loved years ago. Getting her out safely is one thing, but when it looks like she was the arsonist's target, Bryce realizes he can't just let her walk away again. Especially not while her life is in danger.

She's desperate to escape.

For Megan Bristow, returning to Destiny, Texas was about saying a final goodbye to a dysfunctional family and the memories she's tried hard to bury. She planned to go in, help her mother tie up loose ends, and get out again. When someone makes an attempt on her life, Megan realizes those loose ends are only the beginning of a tangled web, and she's been drawn right into the center of it.

They'll have to put the past behind them.

Only by working together will they be able to figure out who's hunting her and why - before it's too late.

Read Out of the Ashes Today

Want a FREE BOOK?
Sign up for Melanie D. Snitker's
newsletter and get a **FREE** novella!
Sign up today!

SPECIAL THANKS

First of all, I want to thank all my readers for your patience. I intended for Noel's story to come out about two years ago. I canceled the pre-order at the time because I had to step back from writing for a while. At that point, I thought *Marrying Noel* may never actually make it into the world. But the story has continued to take up space in my writer brain, and I decided it was time to get it on paper. It was truly a blessing to write.

Special thanks to Trish Long, Alice Shepherd, Steph Dowlen, and Lisa Lee. You ladies are amazing, and I appreciate you all for reading through an early copy and catching all of those pesky typos.

Most of all, I want to thank my Heavenly Father. This series has been such a huge blessing, and it was a big turning point in my author career. Each book holds a special place in my heart, and I'm so thankful that I've been able to do what I love.

ABOUT THE AUTHOR

Melanie D. Snitker is a *USA Today* bestselling author who writes inspirational romance and romantic suspense. She and her husband live in Texas with their two children. They share their home with three dogs and two terrariums filled with frogs, a toad, and a lizard. In her spare time, Melanie enjoys photography, reading, training her dog, playing computer games, and hanging out with family and friends.

https://www.melaniedsnitker.com/

BOOKS BY MELANIE D. SNITKER

Danger in Destiny

Out of the Ashes

Frozen in Jeopardy

Beneath the Surface

Caught in the Crosshairs

Running from the Past

Brides of Clearwater

Marrying Mandy

Marrying Raven

Marrying Chrissy

Marrying Bonnie

Marrying Emma

Marrying Noel

Love's Compass Complete Series

Finding Peace

Finding Hope

Finding Courage

Finding Faith

Finding Joy

Finding Grace

BOOKS BY MELANIE D. SNITKER

Love Unexpected Complete Series

Safe In His Arms

Someone to Trust

Starting Anew

Healing Hearts

Calming the Storm

I Still Do

Don't Kiss Me Goodbye

Sage Valley Ranch

Charmed by the Daring Cowboy

Welcome to Romance

Fall Into Romance

A Merry Miracle in Romance

www.ingramcontent.com/pod-product-compliance
Lightning Source LLC
Chambersburg PA
CBHW032140170626
46808CB00006B/2317